praise
nothing but

'Far beyond the body Lawless takes us to the hypnotic anxiety and ecstasy of a mind that will not relent. You will not regret the ride.' **Yael Stone, actor**

'Tilly Lawless has managed to distill a perfect essence of authenticity into her novel—full of moments of raw honesty, powerful intimacy and memories that leap off the page and into the reader's mind. I was left with certain stories echoing in my mind for days afterwards. A crash course in the delicate nature of human relationships.' **Etcetera Etcetera**

'I inhaled this book in one sitting. Tilly's stream of consciousness crackles with honesty, vulnerability and heart. A captivatingly rendered love letter to friendship, the world we live in, and choosing life, in spite of it all.' **Yassmin Abdel-Magied, author of Yassmin's Story**

'Dirty, smutty, tender and beautiful, Tilly Lawless' *Nothing But My Body* is masterfully crafted stream-of-consciousness poetry punctuated by real-life scenes of Tilly's life. A must-read that will remind you of all the most joyful times of your life while holding you through the pain of the tougher ones. A true gift.' **Nevo Zisin, author of Finding Nevo**

'So intimate, and yet so immense. A sweat- and tear-soaked love cry to contemporary youth, friendship and queerness. From a girls' room in Sydney, to a filthy dancefloor in Berlin, to the creek banks of Northern NSW, Lawless transforms every environment into a playground of fresh questions and heartfelt honesty.' **Brenna Harding, actor and activist**

'A poetically uncensored tour through Australian queer culture, sex work, womanhood and a world on edge. You won't put it down. Captivating, gritty, authentic and relatable. A must read for the girls, gays and theys.' **Ailie Banks, author of *The Book of Bitch***

'An absolute knockout. Lawless writes with such fresh determination and joy. I tore through this for the sex but made myself slow down for the philosophy and deep thinking.' **Bri Lee, author of *Eggshell Skull* and *Who Gets to Be Smart***

'Carnal, aware and magnetic—Tilly's literary flex and ability to carve out intimacy in surprising moments radiates from screen to page and into the body.' **Amrita Hepi, choreographer and artist**

'Tilly writes from the deepest parts of herself. *Nothing But My Body* is unflinching, warm, cool and big. Tilly's goal isn't to prove anything to anyone, she's just telling us what happened and how it felt, but in the process she's given us something deeply tangible, personal and special. You know you're reading something significant. This is a story you'll be reading the rest of your life.' **Caitlin Stasey, actor**

'*Nothing But My Body* reads like a long talk with a friend that I didn't want to finish. Tilly allows access into her world in a way that is incredibly intimate and unflinching. Never rose-tinted, her writing paints a picture of the complexities of mental health, love and identity. A really special book that will stay close to my heart.' **Celeste Mountjoy, @filthyratbag**

nothing but my body

nothing but my body

Tilly Lawless

ALLEN&UNWIN
SYDNEY·MELBOURNE·AUCKLAND·LONDON

First published in 2021

Allen & Unwin
83 Alexander Street
Crows Nest NSW 2065
Australia
Phone: (61 2) 8425 0100
Email: info@allenandunwin.com
Web: www.allenandunwin.com

 A catalogue record for this
book is available from the
National Library of Australia

ISBN 978 1 76106 514 9

Set in 13/20 pt Monotype Garamond by Bookhouse, Sydney
Printed and bound in Australia by Griffin Press, part of Ovato

10 9 8 7 6 5 4 3 2 1

*To all the friends who have listened
to me cry and made me laugh*

saturday

saturday

ENLISTING THIS EIGHTY-YEAR-OLD CLIENT TO TAKE PHOTOS of me. I'm surprised he even knows how to use an iPhone. He's excited, thinking they're for his benefit. He's already slipped me his email, even though it's against the rules – but who am I kidding, everyone does it. He's wanting to banter with me about it; I want to say, Mate, don't forget, this is a customer service job. You might be a sweet client, and by that I mean an easy-client-who-tips-well client, but you're still a client and I don't bother with photos for clients. Don't forget, mate, that though you see me as nude, naked of clothes and context, I am in fact crackling with emotion, a cellophane snap clinging to me from my personal life. That's how I came to be sobbing in this room two weeks ago while a client fucked me in doggy. He hadn't done anything wrong, mind – he was a sweet client, and by that I mean an easy-client-who-tips-well client – but a Teyana Taylor song came on that got me good, and I pretended I was gagging to be pounded so I could have my private mourn into the massage parlour table. He didn't know; thought my shoulders shuddered with pleasure, I suppose. Just like you don't know that my orgasm just then was fake, that I was watching the clock in the reflection to time it out perfectly, that while your head was between my legs I winked at myself in the mirror, as if my reflection was another working girl who was in on the joke. Hey girl, I said to myself, you're going good, you're looking good, you're moaning good, you've got a lot to offer the world and with this old man you're hitting $360 – not bad for a Saturday day shift. And then I counted the money again, realised my moan had turned into a metronome, had a beat like the monologue in my head, and I needed to stop flirting with my reflection and come already. Mate, you wouldn't even know that last time my orgasm with you was really real, that I was disgusted that I managed to come even through the dusting of dandruff falling on my torso, that I wanted to scrub my clit off with a rock, expunge your saliva from where your mouth had sat like an engorged tick. So, mate, you really have no idea, mate, what is going on in my head at the moment — just take the bloody photo. So I can look hot on my Instagram, coz I've already spent enough time playing hot for you.

He takes them. They're okay. I might post one later, if I'm up for the interactions that follow. I selfie less than I used to. For such a long time it was a part of my daily life. At fifteen I took photos of myself to send to strangers online, sounding out my sexuality and coming to terms with my body as a 'desired' object, awkwardly posing in an attempt to be alluring, digital camera on self-timer, background more interesting than me. At eighteen, it was a way for me to reclaim that same body from the touch of men on the street, a way I could assert my control over it and block those who made me feel vulnerable within it, when in the real world you can't block, you're so often at the mercy of, scared. Through my uni degree I selfied as a form of procrastination, just as I masturbated far more than I ever have before. In my single early twenties I sent photos to entice, to feel excited and build a flirtation with a person, to feel a thrill of power with the exposure, knowing that they wanted me and I was gifting them with the knowledge that I wanted them too — it was simply foreplay.

3

In the last few years I've stopped taking them. Don't feel the desire or the need. Why not? Is it because I'm in a relationship and don't need the validation? But I never thought selfies were about vanity or insecurity; they were a form of self-expression. (I don't masturbate anymore either, because I use clients to satiate me, close my eyes and come on their cock if it's an okay shape and they're not fucking me too badly.)

The irony is that it's weakened my words, because without a 'hot' photo of me to interest people, my posts are less likely to show up in people's feeds due to the awful algorithm. Instagram deletes a woman for nudity but encourages us to post thirst traps to be seen. I just can't be bothered with them, though. I see enough of myself reflected in buildings as I walk through the city to a booking, or in the mirrors of a brothel room. I feel sickened by the oversaturation of images, just as I am deadened by compliments after years of being showered with them by men I do not care for. My body has been a tool that I've wielded, but it's also something I just live in every day, that I'm comfortable with and no longer itch to record in order to assert my personhood on the world. I can't tell if that means I'm missing a curiosity I once had, or if it means I'm feeling satisfied in ways I wasn't before.

So what does it mean that I'm now asking a client to photograph me so I can post it online? Am I finally recognising that my relationship has come to an end? Is this me subliminally shouting that I'm single? Have I reached the closure I was unable to reach in that cursed tarot reading, when I just wanted someone to tell me if I should stay with her or not, and instead that Catholic scammer told me I would meet a wonderful man in the next year and have three children with him? 'I'm gay,' I cried, 'and none of this makes any sense! I don't even like gardening.' (The tarot reader had also seen me running a whole-foods market from my backyard.)

Oh, time's up! He showers and I ask him about his plans for the rest of the day while I replace the towels and mop up his mess. My wrist aches, that old RSI inflamed from pulling him off – I really need to move back to brothel work, which will mean looking up brothels I haven't worked at before as I can't bring myself to go back to any of those other ones, the idea of those fell places now sickens my soul – but my mind is on that same tired track it always is. What should I do, what should I do? I love her and I want to be there for her but she's frozen me out, won't

5

even touch me (I touch myself, soaping between my arse cheeks to ready myself for the next client, don't forget the sperm on my stomach, don't want to have to scratch it off, a dried snail trail, while I blow the next guy), till I crave the touch of strange men just for the illusion of intimacy, and then I hate myself, it's pathetic, and wild and sad that you can feel more alone in a relationship than you do outside one. (What's he saying? What days do I work? Oh yeah, babe, just call and ask for Maddy.) And worse than that is the gambling. How can I make a life with someone, have children with someone, who I can't rely on not to spend it all, up in the early morn, crouched over the pokies, intent on them in a way she never is with me anymore, reaching a relief in their depths that I wish she could reach in mine, wish she would skewer me on her fist like she once did and chant into my loins that she would never let anything happen to me, but her addiction is happening to me and she can't protect me from it because she can't protect herself from it. But I don't want to desert her when she needs me and it's about being there for each other during the tough times and putting the other person first and –

'Oh, look at that, it's a beautiful day out there! Have a lovely rest of your afternoon, mwah mwah.'

It's always disorientating when you see the outdoors during a shift. Massage parlours are only ever lit by artificial light. I don't know whether it's too great a privacy risk to have windows letting in the sun, or it's meant to trick the clients into thinking it's night-time and the sordid infidelities they commit will be somehow concealed from the daytime glare, or it's an alternate universe, like the cinemas where you go into those dank, dark rooms and crunch spilt popcorn under your feet and copulate in the back row and emerge squinting into the light.

Did she call intro? Must have – they're all putting their shoes on back in the girls' room. Unfolding numb legs from beneath flannelette robes, switching from Batman boy legs to lace thongs, tottering fawnlike on towering pleasers, ready to please. The Pakistani woman who pretends to be Persian comes back from the intro saying she's seen him before. 'Oh really – what's he like? . . . Oh, what a cunt! Did you tell her? You know not paying for an extra is legally rape coz, like, you guys had an agreement for consent and he didn't stick to it . . . Yeah, I'd get why you didn't wanna make a fuss. If he picks me I'll make sure I get the money upfront. Thanks for telling me.'

I head down the hallway to the intro room; fuck, it's FREEZING! They really need to have central heating not just heat the individual rooms. Like, how can we be expected to wander around in lingerie in the middle of winter? At least my nipples look good, none of that cow teat, thank you very much. Goddamn, the girl ahead of me is taking so long, what are they even talking about? Talk in the room not the intro. Here she is, finally, my turn.

'Hey, I'm Maddy! You have any questions? No, babe, I don't do natural and neither should you. You know things can get passed from throat to penis. Lovely to meet you!'

It's steaming in the girls' room and someone's perfume is giving me a headache. Eight bodies makes it close, and the heater on with the door closed makes it even closer. The two Thai girls are watching make-up tutorials and chatting. They're two of the prettiest girls I've ever seen in my life, and if the modelling industry wasn't so tilted towards whiteness and thinness they would be famous and wouldn't be here. The Venezuelan woman – who is forty-seven but looks thirty-three (sex workers really do age better; is it the cum or the coconut oil?) – says he's walked.

'He's walked? Fucking time waster.' The Bosnian glama has terrifying tattooed brows and rock-hard tits, both done ten years ago, when the fashion was for obvious artifice.

'It is because none of us would give him what he wanted.' The Estonian fitness fanatic – what's she doing here? I thought she didn't work when other Eastern Europeans were on. Or maybe it's just the Russian girl who she avoids; they despise each other, warring over seating arrangements and issuing blunt criticisms of each other's outfits and bodies. What centuries-old country rivalry is channelled through their competitiveness? Or is it purely a person-ality clash, no one but me considering where they came from?

Normally I could fall asleep in here, but I'm so wound up with what's going on at home, wondering where she is, if she's woken yet, if she's eaten, if she's okay, that my anxiety is zapping me awake even over the soporific waves of the heater. The ends of me *teeetch* like a bristling cat. Clients can be simple in their tastes but not so simple that they don't pick up on the static. What cock wants to rest in that? I might be wearing war paint on the outside, but inside is a panic that screeches louder than a brash red. Where is she what is she doing is she okay when will she answer my text — the questions coil around my mind. What do I do should I stay with her should I break up what if I regret this I CAN'T DO THIS ANYMORE I don't want to be dead but I don't want to be alive oh god why can't someone just tell me what to do tell me can I help her can I save her how much longer will it be like this or should I step away save myself —

'What? Oh no, I'm fine, thanks — don't like lamingtons. Yeah, it's the coconut: reminds me of dick. Can't even drink coconut water; tastes like watered-down sperm to me now. Thanks, Baby Bird . . . Oh, it's my joke name for her, coz Aussies can't pronounce her Thai name and the way they say it is like the Thai word for baby bird. But Baby Bird sounds the cutest, don't you think?'

Okay. I gotta calm myself. Think about this rationally or I'm going to break. Breathe in, breathe out. My mind is a fog. Has she texted yet? I need a booking just to get me away from myself. But seriously, how can I bring children into this scenario? How can I inflict this stressful situation on them when I can't even handle it myself? I have an obligation to my future children, don't I? Obligations to myself, too — didn't I say I would never date another addict? That's all I go for. Hot addicts. My friend

was right when she said I was repeating the para-
digm I learnt in my youth, with a charismatic but
financially irresponsible father, in all my romantic
relationships. Gotta break that pattern, for the future
generation as well as for myself.

'What's that? Booking at three o'clock? Thanks.
Oh, slow sex. Yeah, that's David – white guy David.
He drives me crazy but the money is good.'

That'll take out an hour and a half of the day,
one terrible chunk of time gone. Sometimes I feel
like it's time I'm fighting with, having to endure. It
stretches ahead of me, unending hours that I have
to live through. Hours of waiting in which I bite the
skin around my nails to shreds. Waiting for a text
from her. Waiting till she comes home. Waiting for
the dregs of her time, any little bit of attention she'll
give me, direct eye contact or a touch on my arm.
I'm iced out and put on ice, a meal for her to enjoy
when she decides the time is right, but it never is.
The only thing I look forward to is sleep, but even
then I'm waking every few hours to find her still not
there. 2 a.m. . . . 4 a.m. . . . 6 a.m. . . . Will she ever
sleep? 8 a.m. and I'm up for work again, and I have
to get through thirteen hours till I can sleep again.
And she's not even home yet. Sometimes I won't see
her for days; she's turned into a nocturnal beast. But

11

I know she's been home because of the trails and nests around the house, allowing me to trace what she's done. The paintings have been taken off the walls and are on the floor; presumably she meant to rearrange them but didn't finish the job. A knife on the living room floor. Wet clothes in the dryer that hasn't been turned on.

Setting it all to rights, drying her clothes, folding them and putting them away, becomes a labour of love. I can't nurture her in person, I get no time with her, so I nurture and pay tribute to her through my actions. I ready the house so when she chooses to come home she doesn't come home to the mess she left. I hope she sees in that how much I love her. I won't tell her I did it. I don't want anything in return. I just want to do something for her, and this is the only thing I can do. But, oh, these tasks get done and I'm still alone in the house. Not knowing where she is. Not wanting to walk up to the pub to see if she's at the pokies, because I don't know if it'll make me sadder that she is there or sadder that she's not. So many hours to live through yet. I begin thinking about death simply because it seems an escape sweeter and longer than sleep. I know it's not healthy to be thinking of it, and I hate myself more for my lack of stoicism. People have endured far more than this! Friends say, You shouldn't have to put up with this, you shouldn't be in a one-sided relationship, if it makes you this unhappy there's no return in it for you. It's not about should or shouldn't, though. It's about can or can't. And I can endure it. So I keep enduring it.

Work makes me feel normal; it's become escapism when it used to be what I needed to escape from. I can't tell if there's a real irony or serendipity in that. In stepping outside myself to play the bright and bubbly girl next door, in stepping into the physicality of it that is so familiar to me after so many years, I find solace. I like the chatterers who don't give me a second's silence in my head. I hang on every word, the world's best listener. Time passes. Till I come to, with their dick deep, nudging at my depression, and I bite my hand to prevent myself yelling *stop* because that would be unprofessional, and besides I'm not yelling *stop* at them, I would be yelling *stop* at everything, my whole life, because I can't bear any of it, not just his dick inside me – if anything, his dick inside me is okay, it's a distraction, at least it was as it built to an orgasm, sensory overload temporarily easing my panicked thoughts, but then I came and he kept going and he's no longer talking to me so my mind is full again of my own most hated thoughts, and I want him out of me but he's paid for the time and I consented to it and it's not his fault I'm actually suicidal and he doesn't know I want to be dead not just at this moment but many moments so I'll just bite my hand and hope he comes soon and how much time is left?

Slow David is a real mind fuck, too, because he's a slow fuck. Likes to string it out as long as possible, likes to edge with my hips pushed into his – 'Stay still,' he whispers if I move them. He's losing himself in me, the feeling, I get it, but I'm steadily losing my mind in the stillness. It's like the stillness of yoga, and I try to think of what that yoga teacher said the other day: 'Think of the vastness of your mind and the way when you are anxious it becomes smaller. Think of getting back to that vastness. Imagine that vastness.' And I remember how earlier today I read that 'anxiety' derives from a Latin word meaning 'to narrow'. And I know that this is exactly what my mind has been going through: a narrowing. And I know that when I write my mind feels like an immense playground that I can endlessly swing in, with so much space and wonder. And that when I am anxious I tread the same tired paths that wind smaller and tighter, and I lose all my perspective. But I can't empty my mind when I can't empty my pussy, and it's too intimate, this stillness with him inside, an intimacy that I haven't even had with her in months.

There's forty minutes left, I can hardly do it, but if I make him come in ten then leave fifteen for us both to shower he can leave fifteen minutes early and he'll just have to cop that because otherwise I'll crack the fantasy facade that is as flimsy as a mantle of dandelion right now, hardly in place, a firm shrug could dislodge it.

And he's done and I'm out and what do you mean I have another booking right now, a forty-five? That's another forty-five minutes I have to hold off crying when the tears are already pushing against my throat and the back of my eyes, a force that must be reckoned with at some point. No, this is good. Better than sitting around for the last two hours of the day; then I would definitely panic. Get back that girl who winked at herself in the mirror, who felt a surge of power with his head between her legs, even as she felt disgust as his mouth dribbled chocolate-y water from his drooping lips, unable to hold in his sweet treat with any certainty anymore, mixing sweet treats, hope I don't get thrush from it.

'Heyyyy, I don't think we've met before – I'm Maddy! Did you want to hop in the shower? There's a towel for you there. How's your day been? . . . Oh, having a well-deserved break then! . . . Yeah, it's been a bit slow today, but Saturdays usually are. What is it that you're studying? . . . Oh cool. Yeah just chuck the towel there and you can lay face down here . . . No, I don't have to if you don't want; just lie on your back and I can body slide you like this.'

Staying well and upbeat, this is good, rubbing oil on my tits, thank god he wants to chat, slide them across his penis . . . It's still a bit soft — maybe we should stop talking.

'I'm twenty-six, what about you? . . . Yeah, I thought you were around my age. Did you grow up in Sydney? . . . Oh, I've been to Delhi! I enjoyed it but I got real sick, ha ha.'

Damn, he's still soft. Play with it a bit, reverse body slide, put my pussy in his face, tempt him.

'Were you wanting anything else today, like extras? Well, pussy touching is fifty dollars, blow job is fifty and full service — which includes both of those — is a hundred and fifty. Oh no, that's all good, we can just stick with teasing — this is fun as it is.'

Damn, I've gotta fill the time with just this! And he's still not getting hard. Moan a bit but it sounds awkward when he's a deflated balloon in my hand. It's wild to me that men base their ego on something so unreliable, that fluctuates so much in size, far more changeable than the moon which governs our cycles. Is *that* your manhood? Completely unpredictable yet at the same time dully predictable for me, that they'll try to jam it in soft anyway and it's like threading a rope through the eye of a needle while I try desperately to hold the condom in place, a bag of air not cock.

'Wait, what's wrong? You can't get who out of your head? . . . Oh, a girl . . . No, that's okay, you can talk about her, we can stop . . . Oh no, so were you, like, seeing each other? Talking online every night till two in the morning? Yeah, I can see why you thought that was heading somewhere. Fuck, man, that sucks. I do exactly the same thing, though – like I invest so hard in people when they haven't made it clear that they're into me and then end up devastated. These days I just say straight up, like, *Hey, I'm into you, cool if you're not, but just wanting to know where you stand so I'm not, like, projecting on to you and making something out of nothing.* People respect that approach. Plus it makes you look super confident. But yeah, don't be embarrassed. It takes a while to get over stuff like this. Like, more than getting over her it's getting over the imaginary future you invested in, and also the habit of talking to and thinking of her. Trust me, fast forward six weeks and you'll be fine.'

This is great. I love this.

'Oh no, this isn't a bother to talk about at all! Honestly you're talking to the best person about this, I do this *all* the time. I'm such a sucker for romance, and girls especially . . . Yeah, I date women mainly. So I get you. I'm glad this has made you feel a bit better! Honestly, you'll be sweet, it just takes time. And next time just ask earlier what their vibe or, like, intent is, you know . . . Did you still want to come? . . . Yeah, we've still got time.'

Okay, down to business, more oil for his cock. No problem getting hard now. Wow, I really am like a therapist. The most hands-on therapist. If only I was good at taking my own advice maybe I wouldn't be in such a dire scenario – don't think of that now! Wild that it's more socially acceptable for a man to book a sex worker than a therapist, though.

'Pinch your nipples? Yeah, I can do that. Harder? Cool. Slap it – like that? Mmmm, yeah, that's hot.'

He wants me to pinch his nipples, slap his cock and spit on it all while wanking him off, which takes impossible coordination and an impossible number of hands to master, so I'm circulating between them. Got five minutes left till I need to put him in the shower. Okay, this is great, as long as my right wrist doesn't give way. Pause, slap, switch to the left, pinch. Left keep going, right pinch, spit, encouraging moan, slap. Left wrist is no good, it won't get him there, doesn't have the strength or rhythm. Switch back to right – fuck it hurts – left pinch, slap, spit, slap, moan, moan more, get him there faster, faster, before right wrist fails. He's pulsing in my hand, almost there, cup balls, out of hands, bite nipple instead, slap, moan (that was more like a strangled gasp) and there he is! I'm sure I'm almost as ecstatic to see that spurt as he is. Get a tissue, wipe him up . . . This can surely only be a hooker thing, a dead giveaway in a one-night stand; I doubt civilians are doing this for men, so solicitous. *This* is the full service people speak of, it includes cleaning –

'Well that was fun! Just lie there for a moment and get your breath back; I'll shower first.'

Okay, so now it's quarter past five and I finish at six, which means I'll be home in an hour and fifteen, and in an hour and fifteen I'll maybe get to see her – oh god I hope she's home, or at least I'll know if she's home or not. Is she okay? What if she's in bed still, hasn't left all day, doesn't talk to me, pushes me away if I go to touch her – can I handle another night of that? Why am I thinking of myself in this; it's so much worse for her living like that, being unable to get out of bed. What hurts, though, is when she does get up but it's not to spend time with me it's to spend time with the pokies or game with that woman at her house till 3 a.m. and I'm at home having kept my night free in hope but it's always disappointed hope, night after night. Let's hang, I say, it's been two weeks since we've seen each other, we've been passing like ships in the night and me your cabin boy, there to scurry and serve and avert my eyes because my need is something I am ashamed of, and you say, Yes, Thursday night, and then on Thursday you're not home and I finally get a call through to you and you say, Come hang with me at the pub, and I walk up and you're playing the pokies and you want me to sit with you and chat and watch you play and that's what our date night has become when you wooed me so hard at the start, breakfast in bed, devoted conversation, delight in me and now –

'Oh, good luck with everything. Trust me, you'll be fine in a few weeks, she'll be gone from your mind. See you!'

What a lovely boy. Now it's back to the girls' room. The girls' room. That mysterious space, mystical and mythical, dreams of a pink and plush room, when in reality it's scuffed pillows to go with my ageing labia. The girls' room's my favourite place because only the workers see it, and it's where the true intrigue, drama and passion occur. Civilians obsess over the work rooms, what happens there, is it real or unreal, is it hard is it traumatic is it enjoyable, not knowing that it's the most mundane part. That it's just a series of small-talk question prompts, performative compliments, skin dry from too many showers, sticky lube handprints on the suede headboard, sexual need a warm deposit in latex tip or sprayed across breastbone or haunch, dying embers of a lust that didn't last (thank god, my pussy sighs, relieved, and burps out air that was jammed against my cervix). That the real of the real, where I've fallen in and out of love and wonderment and terror and joy and awe and oh god how'll I make my rent nail-biting desperation and the worst things ever said to belittle you by a brothel madam and the cocoon of solidarity and support and a taloned hand reaching carefully inside to remove a sponge – all of that's in the girls' room. That I both hate and miss, that I roll my eyes about and go back to, that I laugh raucously in, under condescending signs that scream: *LADIES, no one is here to hear your sob story so get on the pity train back out of here xo Management* and: *LADIES, don't forget this is a shared space so clean up or you will be fined* and: *LADIES, don't lend anyone money because no one in this industry can be trusted* and: *LADIES, if you see a client privately we will personally make your life and his life traumatic and difficult and you will be fired immediately* when they should say: *LADIES, you're here as an independent contractor not an employee but we'll treat you like a child, our helpless child, till we turn against you and step all over you but make sure you look like a goddess that whole time LADIES because we make money from you being worshipped.* And I might sound bitter because I am bitter about that, but I'll go back anyway because I can't get enough of the girls' room, that space that can't be imagined but only lived. And I've no relationship with my mother so I crave being taken under the wing of the older workers who chain-smoke, and I'm gay so I crave being flirted with by the butch in femme drag who chain-smokes, and I don't smoke but I'll sit in the stale nicotine stench of the smoking area all the same, just to soak it up. Every. Last. Slop.

Except it doesn't look like a refuge now, it feels like a place where I'll be exposed. Forty minutes to make pleasant conversation and avoid eye contact, so they don't ask and I don't cry. Except that goddamn woman is out of her booking. The British one who talks at you even when you put in earphones and pull out a book. A constant monologue – one that I'm not even being paid to listen to! Even more vital to avoid eye contact; don't want to set her off by letting her think I'm her audience. Everyone has their heads determinedly down, looking at their phones, careful not to cue her into beginning. If I hear about Isabella's school project one more time . . .

I can feel it there too, panic, wedged so solidly beneath my epidermis that it is perhaps my epidermis, I'm made of panic, and it's ready to do a foul rosebud exposé, show my insides to the world, just as it did a few weeks ago when I was on that stage and opened my mouth to speak and the lights became very hot on my skin and I started to prickle all over and my hands began to shake and I realised suddenly that there was nothing I could do to stop myself crying, gasping, in front of all these people, it was inevitable. I had a panic attack on stage and fumbled my way off with everyone watching me. That's what it's like now; I need to prepare for any assault, practise my response, breathe. Need to be able to say, Yeah, yeah, it's all good, nothing new happening, same old. Need to be able to lie, to divert, to dissemble. Recite the answer in my mind like the crunch of abs in training, till it's muscle memory in my cerebrum, just a mantra that means nothing and doesn't shake my vocal cords. Yeah, yeah, it's all good, nothing new happening, same old.

Twenty minutes till home time. The girls are all impatient, beginning to pack their things slowly, wanting to go home to their children and partners. Everyone knows if you pack too fast – change into your civilian clothes too soon – you'll jinx yourself and a man will come in and book you for an hour at 5.55 p.m. So we take our time. Put away the food containers from the fridge. Condom bag away. Laptop closed. Take most obvious whore make-up off. Towels down laundry chute. Don't move too fast or you'll invite the ire of whoever looks over us, scoffs at and scorns to think we could predict what will happen in life, predict even the next half-hour. Human ego always readying itself for the next step when we live in a batter of the unexpected, just whisked around at someone else's whim.

And I'm out. Thermal top on, track pants on, Reeboks on. 'Bye! See you all on Monday!'

I'm in my car, and as the 1997 engine starts to shake with the turn of the ignition, vibration up through the floor and the gearstick in my hand, I begin to shake also. Get out of the garage, just drive, break down when you get home. But I can't stop the sobs racking me, it's 'Build Me Up Buttercup' on the radio and as it gets to the chorus I pull on to a side street because I can hardly see anymore and I certainly can't breathe. I can't keep going like this. I've told her, but I don't think she realises that I'm barely holding on by the skin of my teeth. Went to throw myself in front of a bus the other day, and ended up crying in an alley behind Macquarie Street instead, distraught that this was what I had come to when I'd promised myself my mental health would never get that bad again. Where is my resilience, my fortitude? I'm all meekness, insipidness. Where has my backbone gone? I know: I ripped it out like a string of pearls to give to her in devotion, jag upon jag of bone. And now she gambles with those same bones, knuckle rap on the machine, coin clink down that insatiable crevice. I want her to fill me up like she fills up that machine; instead I cry the milky wet of ovulation down my legs, oiled up and unloved, not even another body in the house to bump against in the hall, or a hug thrown to me as one might throw a bone to a dog as you desert it.

My head is both heavy and light in the aftermath as my sobs begin to lessen. Okay, I can drive home. Home, where I don't want to be because every space is reminiscent of her but devoid of her presence. Nowhere else to go, though. Don't want a friend seeing me like this, knowing how bad it is. I still instinctively curl over her in protection, a centipede saving the most beloved part of its self: 'us'. Won't badmouth because that's disloyal. Just say it's difficult but it'll get better. Don't mention the real low because they'll worry, and you don't want to distress them.

Home and she's not there. I need a drink. No alcohol in the house since I quit four years ago. Forget determination, I'm propelled up to the bottle-o by an overwhelming need. Whisky.

Haven't eaten dinner – all the better, it'll obliterate me faster. Have a shot. Have another. Pour a glass, straight; pour a bath, hot. Lock the bathroom door now while I'm still sober so she can't disturb what I'm going to do here. The knowledge is formless in the back of my skull right now but I know it's there, just as I know there are razors in the bathroom cabinet and nail scissors I can use to hack the plastic guard off. I can feel a haze beginning to obscure my mind and my fingers start to fumble with the taps. The sweet oblivion of drunkenness is coming for me. I lie back in the bath to greet it.

Swish, swill, swish. The water feels heavy just like me. She isn't home, who cares, I don't, I don't care what she does with her life anymore. Liquor down my chest. Lick it up – oh, my tongue doesn't reach. Ha ha. Lucky I'm in the bath already. Swish, swish, slap. That slap was good; the water is fun to hit. Stir, stir, slap. Bet she wasn't expecting that, thought I'd keep spinning her around my body in the bath. Stroke, slap, stroke. She's gotta be on her toes with me, I'm gonna beat this water around the bath. Swish, swish, stroke. There's something I don't like, what is that I can feel, is it an emotion that shouldn't be here with me, no no I just want belligerence and disregard beside me. And this whisky, you're allowed too – actually, come sit beside me or float if that's what you want to do. Stroke, stroke, stroke. Stroke away the annoying thought: there's no room for you here. Drink drank drunk I forgot how nice this is. Now I'm ready for what I was really getting to. I'll hate myself for it tomorrow but that's a problem for me of the future not me right now. Slop, slip, slop. These tiles are perilous. Where is it? After so long still familiar in my hand. Hey, friend. Hey, friiiieeeeeend. Room is spinning as is my life but you'll centre me. Slit, slice, slit. Whoops! Sorry, thumb, that was an accident. Soak, suck, suck. And you taste sweet. How nice I feel upon a cloud. Little clouds of blood puffing out the soles of my feet too. Might just lay my head back. Very drunk. Soon I'll be sick. Maybe. Lie back for a whiiiiiile.

A

whiiiiiiiiiiiiiiiiiiiiiiiiiiiile.

Is that what's passed? And – coming to –

I'm vomiting into the rose-pink bathwater and I feel the best I've felt in months. Sick-feeling stomach is now sick-making, and I'm purging it all up in toxic upchuck. Fishing around through clumps of food to find the plug and let it all down the drain. The empty sac inside me heaves and it's just bile coming up now because I've bled and spewed out all that emotion. Tallied the bad on my body, one limb a voodoo doll to pin with all my self-hatred and terror so it can't contaminate the rest. Imbue it with all the sorrow from this relationship so it no longer comes sloshing out and ruining my days, all the caring, the disappointment, the expectations and the tender-ness. I feel no turmoil, just the physical reality of my distressed body in the now. Distressed enough that I can hardly breathe between each yak, it's running out my nostrils too; distressed enough that there's no space for my mind to even think. Yoga is meant to embody you but I am truly in myself now. I lay my head on the cold rim of the bath and feel nothing but relief, pungent seeping drool released in a slow trickle from inside me. Stillness.

This stillness will pass, though. Unless I do this every day, a lifestyle I promised myself I would never enter into again. I need to escape, but where? Home. It's a hallowed term in my mind. Tucked beneath the Great Dividing Range, the rainforest encroaches. Diamond pythons in the roof, bats nesting in my cupboard, satin bowerbirds at the fruit bowl, green tree frogs in the toilet, goanna chasing me on the verandah. That green on green on green. Ferns mark soggy bits of ground, a crossing in the creek, the cool place I like to sit. When it rains the house fills with huntsmen and mole crickets. I rush my outdoor shower when the lightning rocks around the valley, thrown from curve to curve in moments of supreme illumination. Each tree cut stark like the backdrop of a cardboard puppet show or a primary school diorama.

People talk about grass in Sydney, but it's only ever lawn grass so they don't differentiate. Heavy-headed wild oats, hated Parramatta, soft-tipped paspalum, emerald kikuyu, fast-spreading bamboo, grass stained with urea, velvety clover, grass patched with scotch thistles ready to bite at your ankles – all these are unknown and unmentioned. What do they know of castor oil plants rising in the sandy banks in the aftermath of a flood? What do they know of casuarinas, cobwebbed with mist in the mornings by the riverside? For them there is no desperate searching for dock leaves to abate the sting of nettles; there are no farmers' friends to be pulled out of school socks every morning; no cuts on hands from pulling yourself up the river on your belly, one handful of reeds at a time. They talk of trees, but you have to search among the houses to find them. Where are the white cedars with their two-toned leaves; the red cedars, a few majestic survivors of the age of logging; the flame trees, erupting on the mountain; the bunya pines that would prick through my clothes when I went to feed the horses; the hoop pines with the letter-winged kites nesting at the top; the jacarandas whose branches held me as I read; the massive fig tree next to my window with the tawny frogmouths, flying foxes and kookaburras? Where are the sour flowers to eat, the lilly pilly berries to throw, the ferns to watch tentatively unfold? Sydney has the saltwater baptism and the eucalyptus cleanse in rain, but it can't give the consolation of home. It may not be the house I grew up in, that's lost to me forever, but my dad still lives in a rental in that area, so I can retreat to the same landscape of my youth. I could curl up in that green and heal. It's only a 530-kilometre drive.

A 530-kilometre drive is too easy to return from, though. I would be back in two days, tail between my legs, eager to make it work, believing that I am only as good as how hard I fight for us. I know this. I have gone down that road too many times before: cried out the back of the truck stop in Coolongolook, had a crisis at that halfway point next to a dam abundant with waterlilies. Strangely poetic that I fought with my first girlfriend at that same truck stop, seventeen and sobbing. Seems it draws more than road trains.

I have to go further. Somewhere not easy to return from. Why not London? The other side of the world. And I have friends there.

I buy a flight for three days' time. I have already cleaned up the mess in the bathroom. Never again. I am not going to burn myself on the pyre of romance, on a future that exists only in my imagination. I text her, my thumb clumsy in its bandaid. I'm leaving for London.

sunday

I'M HAVING A SUPREME MOMENT OF EUPHORIA. EACH STEP I take on the dance floor imprints the world with my mark, as lasting and significant as a hieroglyphic. I have no urge to text her, no desire to hear from her. For the first time in two years my mind is completely unrestrained and it sweeps around the globe, pressing briefly and lovingly against each friend. What are they doing? How are they? The continents appear like playrooms of promise, I can go anywhere, see anyone. Say anything.

I should text that girl, the one in London. *Hey, I've got a crush on you.* It's true, so true, and shouldn't the truth be shared? Proffered like fruit on a plate for the other to do what they like with it? Hope she'll swallow me whole, the tart 'tang a drip from her lips. I'm best enjoyed in summer, I tell you now. When I can lie languorous and nude on a patio with joint in hand. Fuck me slow and feed me grapes. Fuck me brisk so we have more time to swim.

My phone is too slippery to unlock, been jammed down my boot as I've got no bag or pockets. Do a quick check now to make sure everything else is there. Apartment key is way down, a bulge against my ankle. That's a rolled-up euro note of some kind. Ahhh, there's the ket in its cute little plastic top hat. The Germans are so much better at this than us with our saddies that flutter to the floor, lost, till they reappear stuck to a stranger's sweaty arse.

My phone screen has depth to it; the paddocks of home are elongated columns of green as if I could step inside and be within a Grecian temple. Maybe I shouldn't text her. I'm a bit fucked up. Not that it's embarrassing or wrong to text when you're inebriated, but it's not particularly impressive if someone can only confess to a crush when they're out of it. There's no courage in that. Save it till you're sober. A text comes up, *where u?* I text back, *Panorama, meet at toilets.*

Thank god it's not as crowded as it usually is. Guess it's only 4 p.m. and lots are G dropping at Cocktail or frolicking at Teufelssee. I was throwing them up too, but ended up here coz something about the industrial space called to me, I wanted to flounce once more across that mesh cage bridge that always makes me feel like I'm performing in the cell block tango, wanted to graze myself on concrete blocks beneath bamboo, surrounded by bears but not panda bears just the bearded and beloved bears of the gays, gaze away we're all here to be watched, even in the darkrooms it's part public performance, enjoy my enjoyment, etiquette of the exhibitionist, sacrosanct space, kneel at church this Sunday, lick my shoes you dirty dog I peed on them earlier when I crouched over the urinal, the only girl there, why should I have to queue just coz I have a vagina?

It's a sacred space and I love it, love it even though it's imperfect, even though it's rigged against femmes (you've gotta be a techno lesbian short hair and sports bra for the bouncers to see you as queer), even though like everything it's part pretence – the walls of the darkrooms are simply heavy hanging curtains, as I discovered the night lightning struck the building and the emergency lighting came on and the place was just a heaving mass of naked bodies bared to the bulbs, and I could see people's feet beneath the curtains as they fucked and fellated. Here I am, and I'm feeling so much better than when I was here last year. When I'd fled Paris in the middle of the night to escape that man. Paris, the supposed city of romance, Versailles that famed spot of riot and beauty, and for me, now, fear, running crying down an avenue of trees with the man's crunch on the gravel behind me, his soft ugly uncircumcised dick out and flopping. Would you be able to recognise him? the police asked. I could recognise his dick, I wanted to say. I've been trained to recognise them. Clients only become familiar to me once they get naked. I know which are hard and which make me come and which have bad memories associated with them, all from the shape and the size and the pigment and the tilt. Know how they'll twist and hit inside me, know how sore they'll make my wrist.

The last time I was in Berlin I hardly left my friend's apartment. And when I did I was rugged up in jeans and a huge bomber that I could zip up till even my ears and neck were hidden. Didn't want men to look at me, to see even a slip of skin or guess the shape of me beneath baggy clothes. I was traumatised from my three days in Paris. I had gone for a booking, flown over by a rich man supposedly because he had a fetish for facial moles but in actuality because he wanted to spring another fetish on me, without consent, in a city where I knew no one, couldn't speak the language and was vulnerable to him.

What happened? people asked, expecting a sordid tale of rape or stealthing, and that's what I expected too, am always prepared for, ever vigilant. Well, the first day, before I met up with him, I was harassed by a man in Versailles who chased me down an avenue of trees as the crows cawed overhead and there were no other tourists within sight or sound and I was scared, so scared, but I pulled myself together to meet this client later. And he was a real conservative rich prick, but that was okay coz I'm not paid to actually like them as people, and the first day was okay but the second – well, the second I don't even want to remember as the me you know, I want to distance and disassociate myself from it; it's something that happened to the me of the past and maybe that's just semantics but really that's *you*, not me, I'm stepping away from it – so the first day was okay but on the second he asked if you would peg him and you don't normally do that, like, you're pretty vanilla, a Girl Friend Experience but he said he did it all the time, even had his strap-on ready for you, and you figured it would break the monotony of the three days with him fucking you so you said yes and of course you imagined he had prepared himself because you prepare yourself before anal, like, that's basic consideration, but when you slowly pulled out sloppy shit went everywhere, not just on him and the towel you had carefully laid out but on your hands and legs and feet and all over the floor, and that would've been fine, you breathed through it – stay calm, you told yourself, it was an accident, be professional – but as you stood up to get stuff to clean it, he dropped to his knees and sucked his shit off the strap-on and said, I'm your dirty anal whore, I love being your filthy slut, and then tried to kiss you with flecks of shit around his mouth and asked if you would do a brown shower, and as you stepped away in horror you realised it was deliberate, he had wanted scat play but hadn't asked if you offered it or negotiated what rate you would do it for, just relied on the shock in that moment to let it slide – or maybe the shock itself got him off – and you made him get in the shower as you cleaned it up but even after you cleaned it the places where it had been seemed to glow and he came out of the shower with the shit-stained towel tied around his waist, stains visible, and paraded around as if proud of his handiwork and none of this was what you signed up for and you said you were jetlagged so he would go home to his wife that night and then after he left you cried and emailed him saying he had crossed your boundaries and he had rescinded the right to GFE services such as kissing, oral on you, sex, and the booking tomorrow would have to continue just in the realm of fetish and he said you were overreacting coz you were jetlagged and it wasn't scat play just a bit of power play and you said, Dude, you ate your own shit in front of me, and that's when you booked flights to Berlin and left when it was still dark with a suitcase full of euros, shaking because men can spring anything on you anytime and you'll never be prepared for it all.

For months after I was scared to do private work with new clients, because who knew what could happen? They could do anything, something you were completely mentally unprepared for, at any moment. I tried to anticipate but there were too many possibilities, everyone is so unique in their depravity, how could I counter a sudden exposé? And really he had no respect for me at all and that was what scared me most: that clients with no respect for me could treat me in ways I couldn't predict. Respect has a sameness, a conformity to it, but disrespect is varied and alien in its individual manifestation.

No matter; men don't scare me now. Their eyes are on each other here, anyway, or even if they are on me they won't touch me, I move with such a determined tread through the crowd. They'll ask if I wanna fuck and I can say no and then they'll walk off and leave me be, just like I asked that guy last weekend if he wanted to and walked off to dance before he even had time to think about it. 'I don't normally fuck guys but you're really hot so if you're interested let me know coz I'm down.' After being that forward you've gotta give people their space so they don't feel pressured in any way. Besides, the ball is in their court, they can take you up on it if they wish.

And he did wish. I went around to his the next evening and he was a nerd like me, used to RPG online and we could finish each other's sentences about obscure movie facts. 'I don't usually meet up with girls,' he said, 'I'm a bit weird. Often when I'm meant to I stop replying to their messages on the day.'

'So you ghost them? That's not weird — that's the most normal guy behaviour in the world.'

We fucked and I laughed throughout it because it was just so good to be fucking someone out of pure attraction, just because I wanted to, not motivated by money at all. And it was fun, unlike the sex with her by the end, which was heavy with too much emotional emphasis because it so rarely happened and I ended up unable to relax and was tight inside in a way I never had been with her before, coz really it had been so long and I had cried over it so much that when the intimacy finally came it only hurt because it cascaded through my life with light and threw all the shadows, the lack, into relief.

'You're the first guy I've fucked for free in five years,' I said, and he repeated, 'For free?!' and laughed. He had no idea of the significance of it, how it brought me back into my body with joy when for so long I had felt at odds with my body, either ashamed of its wants in my relationship, or only able to access it through the desires of clients. I had written off casual sex as not worth doing for free, because emotional sex was so superior, and truly good sex with someone you're emotionally connected with is the pinnacle of sex, but that didn't mean the pleasures of connecting with a stranger in a moment of genuine physical intimacy should be denied me as a single person.

'Let me know if you come back to Berlin,' he said.

'I will, but I won't be offended if you don't reply,' I said, and he looked surprised and relieved, as if I got something about him, or he wasn't used to someone not holding him to something. I felt like saying, Babe, you gotta fuck a dyke more often. I don't need you for validation and couldn't care less if this happens again beyond the fact that it was fun and I'm always down for more fun. I only hit on you coz I lost the girl I wanted to get with that day somewhere in the club and then met you and thought, *Why not get with this guy with the beautiful face who isn't staring at me creepily and is talking to me as if I'm a person not a girl with her nipples and pubic hair visible to everyone?*

I just ran down the stairs of the darkened apartment building and yelled back at him to hit the stairwell lights so I didn't have to slow my pace because I had a flight to London to catch, otherwise I might've stayed for round two.

Damn, now I'm horny thinking about that, squashed like a sardine into this bathroom stall. 'Guys, I'm so horny I can hardly dance!'

'Here, babe, do this line of K and then I'll do up a line of speed for you, too – that'll fix you, or it'll fix your cunt.'

Yeah, I need to fix my cunt all right. It's an annoyance between my legs right now, heavy with need. Gloating and proud, aware of its power, a searchlight streaming from it, on the prowl. Should've masturbated earlier to ease this, fed my fingers into its greed and let it spit them back out again, satiated slop.

Wow, those lines wipe me. Let the others lead the way back to the floor. Reach out an arm to clasp a mesh waist so I don't lose them in the churning crowd. My feet are square nuisances. Not knives getting sharper and sharper with each step but bundles of lead that I have to drag. I try getting up on the podium but it's too much for me. I need to pee. 'I'll be back soon, guys, or I'll find you to the left of the speakers . . . Yeah, fag hag corner.'

Hold on to the railing on the way down the stairs or I might topple like a broken doll on the heel of my boot. Darkness and smoke clothe me more than anything else, my open-crotch panties baring my labia to the world. Wait, who's this guy coming up the stairs looking at me? Do we know each other? He looks familiar but also not . . . He's looking at me so intently, though, it's going to be so embarrassing if it's a friend I don't recognise. I've slowed to steady myself and oh my god what if it's the guy I fucked last week? He was so nice that it would be rude if I didn't say hi, especially as we fucked sober, in the light. It's not his fault I fuck so many guys — and besides, he wasn't a client, so I would hate to cold-shoulder him. I know there's a way I can find out if it's him or not.

'How was Hamburg?' I ask.

He answers but I can't hear him over the music. Then we're making out and he's finger-fucking me on the stairs. I'm loving it. My body wants this so much. His beard has really grown since last week and he seems to have shrunk but that's just the ketamine confusing me; he's handling my body with such confidence it *must* be him.

Do I wanna go with you? Sure.

In the bathrooms now and still not quite sure if it's him. If we just had a few minutes to chat I could work it out but instead I'm asking if he has a condom coz my pussy is driving this and then he's fucking me in doggy against the cubicle wall and he was able to slide in without any lube, even though condoms would usually cause friction, coz she's just so wet and ready and has been all day, has been all week really. I am loving it. Loving that I didn't even have to pull my underwear down, he could just enter me from behind. Loving that the stall doors are like saloon doors, they finish at your calves and so people waiting definitely know what's up and can hear us. Loving that he's fucking me even harder than last week. Loving that I'm finally having the spontaneous single fuck I've wanted to have here, so the time my ex fucked me in an alcove while I leant against a wanking voyeur as back support is no longer the most salient memory. Loving that after so many years of work sex and relationship sex I am unlocking the slut part of me which had been channelled into the professional but now is mine to revel in. And as he comes his arm reaches around me and with a sinking feeling I see that he has a whole arm tattoo and he definitely did not have *that* last week. And I turn around to him as he chucks the condom in the toilet and ask, 'Do we know each other?'

'No, did you think we did?'

'Yeah, I fully thought you were someone I knew.'

'Who?'

'It doesn't matter.'

I go to leave and he says, 'Here, have some of this,' and gives me a pill to bite. I walk out slightly shell-shocked, splash water on my pussy in the sink in the hope I don't get thrush. Wonder if I consented to that. Wonder where my friends are. Where are they all? I've dragged myself upstairs and they're not here. The gardens shut soon; they're probably there making the most of the outdoors.

Back into the cavernous depths; squeeze through the cattle crush of the downstairs toilets. There they are, sitting next to the ginormous rubber cock. 'Guys guys guys I just fucked a guy by accident or maybe not by accident but in a case of mistaken identity and now I feel all weird about it also coz I was so fucked up I could hardly walk but I could talk and I could fuck, obviously. I used a condom, though, thank god I'm institutionalised like that, so no worries there, but, like, I wouldn't have fucked him if I'd known he was a stranger so, like, what does that mean, is it like consent through deception? . . . Yeah I did enjoy it. And no he didn't know I thought he was someone else, it wasn't, like, calculated on his part. He was just in the right place at the right time, lucky guy, god I should never take speed, I get so horny it's ridiculous, this is why I never touch G, last time I did I was humping my girlfriend at the time while chatting to her without even realising we were in public, so mortifying and now I can't even be trusted going to the bathroom by myself without screwing someone!'

'Babes,' a friend says while peeking into his nostrils with a compact mirror, 'if you thought he was the other guy the whole time you were fucking him, and we all know being turned on is mainly about what's in our mind, then really you were fucking the other guy, so who cares who he really was?'

'Yeah, actually, you're so right and they had the same dick too, both circumcised, similar size, otherwise I would've realised it was a different guy when I put the condom on. Oh great, that's fine then, for a moment I felt sick like maybe I had been assaulted but if I've been assaulted by anyone it's my own mind. Help me up onto this block, will you, please, I'm too fucked up to jump and I wanna sit up here while we smoke a joint, that's what you're rolling, right?'

I have a drag and sigh back against the concrete, grateful to be in Berlin. London held me and let me blubber through her graciously – at a pizza shop in Notting Hill, at a ceramics store in Maida Vale, in an apartment on Gloucester Road, walking to the tube station near Hyde Park Corner – but I always feel so class conscious there. Took my top off at a rich kid's party because it was hot and I wanted to dance more comfortably and forgot how conservative people there can be. I'm so used to the queer party bubble of Sydney and Berlin, where it's normal to take off your clothes once it's over twenty-five degrees and sweaty, and no one comments or touches, that I was shocked by the stares.

I'm trying to work out why being around young people with money makes me so uncomfortable, like when I'm at a party full of people who pay for sex and drugs rather than sell them. People who can borrow money from their parents and who maybe even own their own homes. People to whom a gambling addiction is 'poker' and not the end of the world, rather than the pokies and destitution. Do I feel secretly inadequate? Resentful? Or is it just that the class difference is tangible to me in a way that it usually only is when I'm being handed cash by a client in a bougie hotel? I'm confused by how I, as a working girl, fit in to a world in which another working girl would be hired to hand out shots topless and be treated as a spectacle? A guy there asked me why I still do sex work: 'You know all these people now,' he said. 'You could get a job through them.' I replied that I wasn't into nepotism. It made me realise that I take pride in having taken care of myself financially, and I judge people who haven't, which probably isn't fair because they are just a product of a skewed system, like I am. And pride is often a cover for insecurity anyway, so is that what's really underneath? I could couch my insecurity in the rhetoric of 'eat the rich', but I would rather analyse what it is of theirs that I both hate and want. The stability, the entitlement, the good seat to watch the world burn from?

Berlin feels classless, though of course it's not, and it has its own problems. White queers gentrifying neighbourhoods that have traditionally belonged to Turkish immigrants. Gay clubs unwelcoming of femmes, as if masculinity is the peak of human expression. But in this moment, surrounded by queers who have left hostile countries and made their way along winding, treacherous paths to eventually reach this sunlight of our own conjuring, it feels like a utopia. A Colombian boy and I discuss our intense desire to fall pregnant and become parents, and absolutely anything seems possible as we watch a horde of lithe bodies pour out of the door, with eye patches and bandages and knee supports.

'Why do you think queers are so obsessed with the aesthetics around injury?' he asks.

'I think it's coz historically our bodies are seen as abject bodies – you know, like vectors of disease, ailing and failing, faulty and barren. We just lean into that.'

I don't add that as a sex worker my body is especially viewed so: a vehicle for contagion and public health risk, used and abused, devalued and discarded. I don't add that I want to be fruitful in spite of that, and maybe even because of that. I want to reproduce because people say it's dangerous to and I know it's not. My only fear is that my sins will be visited on my children, that they will be judged because of the labour of their mother, even as she laboured to bring them into this world with the same copper loins that conquered men. I don't want my children to suffer, branded the offspring of a whore, as if this whore hasn't worked every minute with their future in mind. I don't add that I hope they're born into a kinder world that my words have helped to create.

Thinking of bodies, mine is getting restless. Boots beating against the seat, my feet feeling my impatience before my mind is even aware of it. It's time to dance again, for sure. That joint has evened me out and I'm over that blip of confusion, able to think again and even write if I tried, I reckon.

'You guys wanna go dance? . . . Yeah, let's go via the bathrooms. I'm gonna stay away from the speed this time, though – I don't need another misfuck.'

There's a hand on my arm, a straight blonde girl I've met once before who showed little interest in talking to me.

'Oh my god, I heard you fucked that DJ, Fedonev! I want to fuck him too. I'm going to use the same line you did: that you don't normally fuck guys but he's really hot. He never fucks anyone – well done.'

'Um, I said that coz I'm gay and it was true. It wasn't a trap.'

Escape to the bathrooms. It's like a sauna in here, other people's sweat dripping off the ceilings onto me after evaporating up there from them, the circle of life – no wonder we all came away from here last time with that same mysterious sickness, pain in our kidneys, it's like standing in a soup of shared microbes, I'm probably getting the residue of drug intake from someone three stalls down. What a wonderful world, though, and I am happy to be in it. Wonder what the London chick is up to; wonder if she's thinking of me. Probably not. I'm not posh enough for her, just a fascinating distraction in other-ness. A prostitute rubbing shoulders with the upper echelons, how thrilling! Didn't feel like that with that guy last week; I felt as if I met him as an equal. I didn't know who he was, though. If I had, would it have changed anything? I don't think so. I feel confident that I'm as good as anyone else who has got things through talent. I don't feel on the same footing with people who get things through family connections. No matter how smart or articulate or cultured I am, I'll never be able to crack into that world of people whose parents have supped and

holidayed and intermingled for decades and sometimes even centuries. But why would I want to crack
into it? Why do I care?

I do my line off the phone case and tune back
in to the others. They're talking about that girl and
how they can't believe what she said to me, they all
heard it. I can't believe it either, really. But it's got
me thinking. K always gets me thinking, epiphany
after epiphany on the dance floor. My thoughts
swarm out into the cubicle conversation . . . 'It's an
example of the way we enshrine male creative talent
as something that should be worshipped,' I say, 'and
how idolising is often dehumanising, like, while she
thought she was paying him a mark of respect, and
me too, she was actually disrespecting us both.'

'What do you mean?'

'Well, she had no interest in me before I slept with
the DJ, which suggests my worth is somehow tied
to who I sleep with – it doesn't come from within.
This is how women have been valued throughout
history, you know. Groupies, muses, wives – they're
all secondary, known for their connection to the men
whose creativity they inspire and support, not in
their own right, reflected glory rather than basking
in their own, like their work was overlooked for his.'

'Girl, speak!' And my friend drums on the stall wall with his fist, rolled-up note protruding like a business contract.

'Well, this is my craft. Just as there's another DJ working his craft upstairs right now, I'm working mine: words. I guess I've even used my time with him to fuel my own creative flow, if you can describe this monologue I'm inflicting on you like that, in the same way male genius historically has been stoked by women whose own lives or talents are sidelined or sacrificed to that greater objective: his output. That's why it's so insulting: it assumes my value can be changed by associating with someone, not through my own achievements. I also hate it coz it sets up such an awful power dynamic, of the mighty bestowing the glow of association on the lesser, rather than the meeting of two equals, which does both of us a disservice. Reduces him to just a flimsy frame of his DJ persona, reduces me to a foil.'

'Babe, she's a star fucker, and it's sad if that's really where she thinks her worth comes from.'

'Well and that's the other thing! Besides the fact that she talked about how I hit on him as if it were a tactical move rather than a genuine moment of honesty from me, the use of his DJ name rather than his actual name makes me think: do you actually want to fuck the person or the DJ? Like, what is with this complete obsession with artists that leads people to tender them like currency, to collect them like notches in a belt? How do we dismantle this cult of celebrity? And, like, I say that knowing I wield some weird power as someone with an internet following, and I've seen firsthand how "famous" people are no longer treated as who they are but just as what they represent. Like, he's a person beyond his social capital. False idols only fail us, and we fail them in the moment we turn them into an idol, not a person. But I think the thing that upsets me the most is that it tarnishes what was a wholesome experience for me by reducing it to what could be "got" from it. You know, like social capital, guest list, whatever. She spoke as if I had scored something by sleeping with him, like I was lucky. When in reality we were both lucky, just as anyone is lucky to have a mutually beneficial joyful moment of human connection. I wanna say, be happy for me not for who I slept with, but that I slept with someone and I enjoyed it. I thought casual sex was ruined for me and I was wrong, and now the world is full of infinite potential. Isn't it wonderful to meet someone stripped of any pretensions, have some fun and then go your separate ways, knowing the world is full of people you can meet and connect with? I know I sound sappy now and am ranting but, like, if I wanted something from sex besides that moment itself then I would have paid sex – I do that all the time. Actually, maybe that's why I'm so sensitive to it, because I'm, like: Babe, I was off the clock!'

'Just coz you're a whore doesn't mean everything you do is whoring!'

'Exactly. Anyway. Whatever. Thanks for letting me rave, I've got it all off my chest now and the K is hitting me. Sorry for holding us all up from dancing.'

'Girl, never. We loved that. Wish you would say it to her face.'

We heave out of the bathroom into the melee waiting to embrace us, consume us, make us part and parcel of the masses, arms tied tight to our bodies by those all around us. I can feel other people's skin against my skin, a long length of thigh pushed up against mine as our tallest friend shoulders his way through the throng. Night is coming and the club is filling up. Outside, I know, a line of silent trepidation stretches past the kiosk, past the taxi rank, each waiting for the nod or shake of the head that'll define their evening. I think of how sex work has shaped the sex I have in my private life, the fact that I revolt at any suggestion of gain from sex, won't even let someone I fuck buy me a drink or pay for my taxi ride home, in case they think I've come to them as Maddy and not as myself. I think of how in movies the most hurtful thing a lover can do to a sex worker is suggest that what she's been doing out of desire she's secretly been doing for money. That scene in *Moulin Rouge* where he throws cash on her, putrefying what was pure. Is it internalised whorephobia that I'm so determined to have an uncrossable delineation between my private life sex and work sex? Yes, I'm a whore, but only at work. Outside of work I have integrity. Is that what I really think of sex for gain, that it lacks integrity? Or does it lack integrity only when it's not transparently for gain? To say, 'I'll fuck you for this amount,' is fine and honest, but to fuck someone out of feigned interest when you actually have an ulterior motive is not. I think it's the pretence I can't stand.

I'm too much in my head. Need to just immerse myself in the surrounds. Going up the stairs now, god that sounds good. And as we rise up onto the main level a trans girl I know appears before us on the podium completely naked, shaking her hair like a wet dog, and I feel as if we've entered Valhalla. Just bodies and sound, the techno reverberating through the floor, and my mind starts to hear voices in the beat, and the voices are saying again and again as if they're blessing me, *Berghain bitch Berghain bitch Berghain bitch*. And I think, that's right, that's what I am, a bitch who'll suck on your cock and piss in your mouth and fuck you by accident in the bathroom and walk down a street unafraid and give you a fiver to get home and tell you everything on her mind and roll her eyes at a bore of a man and, if you're lucky, spend some time with you and maybe, hopefully, one day, birth a child. The club feels me, it knows I'm here, and I ride on the crest of this crowd, a bitch of the finest order, the crème de la crème of bitches, but no better than anyone else around because shouldn't we all feel our majesty in being alive when we could all so easily be dead? It's a miracle really and I was so close to killing myself and if I had I would never have felt this moment of being.

'Is the music saying anything to you?' I shout into my friend's ear.

'Not right now, but often it says, *ketamine dancing ketamine*, and even when I get home it's still saying that.'

Maybe it's not that profound; maybe I'm just fucked up. Still feel great, though. Wish all my friends were here with me in this moment.

I send a love heart to every single one of them so they know.

One replies immediately: *hahahaha love you. Are you munted? It's 5 a.m. here and you always send a love heart when you're munted lol.*

Well, I am, but it's true all the same. I love them sober and not sober – it's consistent.

There's a guy pushing past me and oh my god it's the guy I accidentally screwed! Now I can see better he really looks nothing like the first guy . . . He's at least a foot shorter, has a beard, so many tattoos . . . The two men wouldn't even be picked for the same police line-up (though their penises would). I guess they're both vaguely Germanic-looking with blue eyes. Wow, I really am a lesbian. If it was a girl I'd banged I would know her face back to front, every freckle, from yearning over her social media.

Wonder what the London girl is up to. The conversation with her is so good that I wonder if we're as compatible in other ways. I'm so over client sex. Vigilant, cervix-spasming, condom-checking, clock-watching client sex. Not that it can't be fun; it can. But I want to have sex with someone I'm into.

I want the bedroom to be an addition, not the purpose. I want to laugh, and then come, and then laugh again. I want to be under, over, in, deep, with someone new. Till we collapse in on each other, forget the time and wake up three weeks later when reality breaks down the fourth wall and one of us has thrush. I don't want someone I just find hot, that I'll let top me but won't let kiss me. I want to fuck and be fucked, to be so interested in them that the sex is interrupted by conversation, and then the conversation by sex. Maybe I just want intimacy, the tactile kind. The getting-to-know-you-from-the-inside-out kind. The three-fingers-deep, mouth-tasting-of-you kind. The I'm-hungry-let's-make-toast-at-three-in-the-morning-so-we-can-keep-going kind. The lesbian kind.

I fantasise about more than a fuck, as nice as the time with that guy was. But I don't fantasise about romance. That desire is deadened for me by the last five years of relationships. Romance serves only romance, a nasty creature consuming itself and both of you in the process. And all that's left is a strap-on you don't want to wear and a t-shirt you don't want to wash.

On the podium to the left of the stage there's a man on his knees giving another man a blow job.

They're right at eye level but gazes just sweep past them to the DJ booth, which was designed to be at ground height to eliminate hierarchy. Because, sure, they're playing for us, but we're dancing for them, and there's an exchange. Just as my writing is brought more meaning by the tears cried by those who read it, so we are making something all together, in our bodies and the spaces between us and the moments in which we touch. In this dark sanctuary where we close the blinds against the sun's rays and dance on as if a new week isn't beginning, where we dance for sixteen hours, twenty hours, twenty-four, and end up too exhausted to leave, just hovering around the entry on peeling leather couches watching other people circulate, see that same girl lap the building, see that same security guard shaking someone awake, see ourselves not at all with a sticker covering our phone cameras and no mirrors to remind us of how gross we are with our possum eyes and gurning troll faces. We stay on because we've been stripped of any semblance of propriety, 'looking good' forgotten, just like that one lone swimmer in the Kit Kat pool, we checked in our inhibitions along with our jackets and now I'm with my muscles and my sinews and that thyroid cyst I push around my throat and the dried cum my pussy has leaked that I can scritch off my thighs with a thumbnail and my mind sharp and demanding and my excitement to live, to be a part of this messy imperfect world, in the fritter of my fingers and the leap of my thoughts across my synapses, quickening with the breach.

monday

SHE'S MOISTURISING HER HANDS AGAIN BUT THEY'RE STILL cracked and flaking — too many years of washing dishes without gloves, she tells me. She started sex work late, when she was already fifty, and now she's nearing sixty and none of the city brothels will hire her. I'm here because I wanted to try a famed mining town; veteran workers always wax lyrical about the amount of cash you can make in places where women are few and men are trapped, too much cash to be believed, too much to fit in your wallet or bra, and so I made the three-and-a-half-hour drive west to this country town that is nothing like the one I grew up in, all dry eucalypts and dust, no rivers to break the heat. A backyard to sunbathe naked in, though; I can lie in the grass between bookings and stare at the one lone palm tree and feel like I'm on holidays. City broths could never!

She wants to move back to Cambodia, she tells me, is trying to make enough money to retire there. But it's hard when it's a race against her age and each year new younger girls appear. I feel that and I'm only twenty-six. I know there's a legion of eighteen-year-olds coming up behind me, have noticed I don't get the clients with paedophilic fantasies anymore; they reserve their whispered smut for the ears of girls much younger and more nubile than me.

Around her the notices shout down at us from baby pink and mint green walls: *TO AVOID CONFLICTS DO NOT TOUCH OTHER PEOPLE'S FOOD GIRLS ARE NOT REQUIRED TO SHARE FOOD* and: *DEAR LADIES IT IS THE RESPONSIBILITY OF ALL GIRLS TO CLEAN UP AFTER YOURSELVES AND KEEP THIS AREA TIDY* and: *ATTENTION LADIES THIS IS A SHARED AREA MEANING NO SLEEPING ON LOUNGE AND NO LAYING DOWN ON LOUNGE WHEN OTHERS WANT TO SIT AND NO SUITCASES, MAKE-UP AND PERSONAL BELONGINGS TO BE SCATTERED ALL OVER THE PLACE!* In spite of this the place is fairly welcoming. We can stay as long as we want with a room to sleep in without having the cost of accommodation taken from our earnings. The management are kind, because being so far from anywhere there's a scarcity of workers and they can't afford to frighten us away. They're actually grateful when we show up, in stark contrast to some of the metropolitan places I've worked at which act like they're doing me a favour for hiring me, forgetting that it's my body that's the drawcard and worksite.

'I have an older woman friend who still works at brothels,' I say. 'I can text her and ask what places in Sydney hire mature-aged women, if you want.'

'Oh, honey, please, if you could – thank you, honey.'

She gets back to me five minutes later. Amanda's Heaven and Cougar Town. Not particularly appealing names, but I've worked at Real Promiscuous Massage and Wives Only so am not in a position to judge. Her mobile has no internet, so I look them up for her and give her their addresses and phone numbers, and as she writes them down she says, 'Thank you, honey, oh thank you so much,' over and over again. I know that relief, the pain of the hunt for money. Not like her, because I'm young and white and can get hired wherever I want, but I have sat on shift after shift where I've earned nothing and racked my brains for somewhere else to go and feared that my time is over and that even sex work, which is meant to be the last resort, is finished for me and I can't even sell that most basic of resources, the one I'm born with. I know the panic. And so I'm glad when the first client of the day comes in and I say no, I don't do kissing, and he picks her instead.

I move outside to get that sun, play on my phone and find myself back on that person's Instagram profile. Count how many photos of theirs I've liked, wonder why they haven't liked any of mine, check out who else they follow and see they've been liking other girls' photos. Are my photos not as good or do they not find me attractive or does the time difference just mean they miss mine in their feed or are they just not interested in me at all? But they always reply to my messages, are happy to chat, and surely that means more than a photo like anyway? Maybe they don't feel the need to engage in that public approval when I'm a sure thing; maybe that's how they court someone and I don't need to be courted. I would rather they replied to my messages and didn't like my posts than the other way around, so why do I feel sad that they're giving likes to others? It doesn't take away from our communication. Still, what does she have that I don't? She's a model, sure, so conventionally better-looking. But I know people find me interesting and compelling, and that's more important in the long run. I know I've fucked a lot of hot people myself but it's the ones who make me laugh that I'm drawn back to.

I know it doesn't matter yet I still obsess over it. Reread our old messages. Scroll back through every photo they've liked. It doesn't thrill me as much as the first time, though, and I want more. Another hit of dopamine, all the way from Europe. Express delivered. Instantaneous effect guaranteed. I could post this photo as a trap, but then if they don't respond to it it'll make me so sad; it doesn't matter if it gets a few thousand likes when the one it was posted for doesn't recognise it. Besides, it's always better when they respond to something of mine I haven't posted for them, when it's unexpected.

'Maddy, intro!'

Brush the grass off, bodysuit and heels on. I'm slightly sweaty but in that nice, wholesome, sun-baked way, just perspiration, like a lady, don't even smell. Inside is cold – the sun won't make it through these old brick walls – and I feel as if I'm striding a solitary catwalk down the carpeted hallways, imagining it is them watching me on the other side of the world, not my doppelganger in this ornate mirror.

The client's a young white guy with a beard and high vis; I bet like most tradies he'll book for halfa and he'll be no frills, simply wants to get off in between jobs.

I'm right and he's out of there in less than fifteen minutes, including both showers. Easily satisfied with small talk and doggy, forgettable in the best possible way. I come back into the girls' room and before I even have time to dance a little jig over the sheer joy of money making I'm called out for another intro and I'm in a forty-five immediately.

He wants me to lie down on my stomach while he slowly kisses up my legs and torso. I momentarily feel bad that I haven't shaved them as he cradles them in his hands and begins to kiss the soles of my feet. 'You are so beautiful, sweetie,' he whispers over and over. Like ASMR it's a soporific and I could almost fall asleep. That soft sibilance . . .

'Are you Iranian?' I ask.

'Yes, I am, sweetie – how did you know?'

'The way you say your S's. I've heard it before in people whose first language is Farsi.'

'You know Farsi? You are smart as well as beautiful, my love,' and he lightly sucks my toes in devotion.

'What is this on your foot?' he asks as he strokes my tattoo.

'It's the postcode of my hometown. I wanted it there so no one would see it, coz it's private to me, but also my sole is what has direct contact with the world in the earth I tread and my left sole is the same side as my heart.'

'Oh! You think of this stuff that is wonderful. I do not always make love with the girls here but I want to with you – you are deep, I can tell from the way you think.'

Usually when clients say 'make love' it makes my skin crawl because they're placing an emphasis on the sex that I don't think it has, intimating that we have an emotional connection. With him, though, I think he just says it because 'fuck' seems too abrasive. I can tell he chooses his words carefully, wanting them to be as gentle as his touch. We end up doing it face to face, sitting up, more rocking our groins together than anything. I stare at his temple between his eyes, a trick of the trade, because from his perspective it looks like I am staring directly into his eyes. He comes quietly and quickly, before I begin to feel violated by the intimacy of such a position.

He cleans himself fastidiously afterwards, even drying his penis with tissues after the shower so as not to dampen his underwear. The crotch of my bodysuit by comparison is filthy, stiff with dried lube and discharge. I let him back out onto the street, give him a kiss goodbye on the cheek, and go into the intro that's already waiting. Another tradie and he picks me for half an hour. So $85 + $100 + $85 = $270. That's good for midday, especially as I'm going to be here till 10 p.m. There's really something to be said for working way out in the country when you're at the only brothel in a two-hour radius and there's only two of you on a day shift. No competition.

Wow, though, this guy is awkward. Doesn't want to chat, doesn't want to make eye contact. He's probably got a wife back home, judging by the ring on his finger. I ride him in cowgirl and he comes in less than a minute, then hurriedly pulls his clothes on with his back to me without even having a shower. I have to rush to open the door for him and he takes off like a bat out of hell, driven by his desire into a place like this and driven out by shame. Is he afraid of me judging him? I wonder. Or does he avoid my eyes in case he sees something human in them, is forced to engage with me beyond an orifice to dispel his semen into, realises that I remind him of his daughters or other women in his life? Maaaate. It's not innately disrespectful to me or the women at home if you pay to fuck me, I want to say. And it's not my business if you're married. I feel for your wife for being cheated on, sure, but I also feel for you for being trapped in a society that promotes sexual monogamy as the only valid form of relationship and won't let you express your desires outside of that. And I get that maybe it doesn't feel like you've betrayed her if you don't talk to me, coz subconsciously we all know it's emotional infidelity that matters. God, there are those who sew up their genitals to everyone but their spouse and have emotional flings with their 'work wife', as if that's somehow better! If only we could all voice our want; if only we didn't quantify love according to level of possessiveness.

I'm hungry now, so I order a pizza and sit in the sun and scroll their Instagram profile again, imagine them being in Australia and how they'd laugh at my old car and then be impressed by how comfortable I am in the city that I've made my own, how I jaywalk in the CBD because I can read the traffic patterns and walk home from the beach barefoot and sandy and am unfazed by anyone staring when I laugh raucously. Think of them finger-fucking me beneath the etching of Frederick the Great, Frederick the Gay, that hangs above my bed and think of them coming north with me and seeing the place that makes me who I am, why I'm unlike other girls they've met because I'm not European and collected; I'm country Australian and brash and as honest as our summer is long.

But they won't come here. I'm not a big enough draw to warrant flying to the other side of the world — at least not when you're European and a long-haul flight seems insurmountable. I used to travel a hundred kilometres a day just for school, my concept of distance honed by the huge continent I come from. I'll put in the effort but they won't, they won't even like my Instagram posts, and here I am taut in my stomach again, fretting over them. Can't even tell if it's anxiety or hunger now; either way it's a bore that I get like this, no fun when the endorphins of a stalk dissipate so quickly, become despair.

The doorbell rings and I go to get my pizza, open the door in my work wear and the delivery boy is so nervous that his hands are shaking as he gives me the change. Poor kid. I'm not going to abduct you. And you're not irrevocably tainted by standing on the doorstep of a brothel; the stain is not that perdurable. Though my extended family see it that way — think I leak a stench from my cunt, have left a mark on the family name that can't be scrubbed out, unlike the stink of a bitch in heat. I guess he's lucky that us whores come in by the back door, that he doesn't have to stand in the pool of muck that seeps from our overused pussies, glorified sewers, pussoirs.

'It's so hard to get a handyman in to fix the broken shower,' the receptionist tells me as I close the door. I don't need to be told. I know how the curiosity is mingled with fear and revulsion; I saw it in his wide eyes.

I'm eating my pizza out in the backyard when I get called in for another intro and this one picks me for a spa booking. I get an extra $20 just to fill the bath and sit in it with him, pamper him beyond the perfunctory. He's a farm boy, sheep not cattle, and he quickly makes his political opinions known. Anti-immigrant, even though neither of us is Indigenous so we're sprung from immigrants ourselves. Anti-gay, though not anti me being 'bi' coz that's hot, but none of that guy-on-guy stuff, thank you very much, and as long as I don't sleep with bull dykes, just other girls like me. Thinks people who are depressed are weak, and no wonder there's such a high suicide rate among men in rural areas I think as I plunge my arm under the water to hide my self-harm scars. Not that I'm ashamed of them, but the last thing I want to do is enter into a conversation about them with a guy like this. I remind myself that I'm paid to placate and please, not to be myself, as I play with his balls with my toes, his penis semi-submerged and wrinkled.

We begin to talk about his family; he's got a crest tattooed on him. They're originally from Wales.

'Wales? Oh, I love Wales! Have you been there?'

He hasn't. This doesn't deter me, though; I mistakenly think that because colonial history fascinates me it'll fascinate him too.

'The thing I love most about it is how they've managed to preserve their language, in spite of being pretty much consumed by the English. Like, in Wales you actually hear people speaking Welsh openly on the streets, which you don't hear so much with Gaelic in Scotland or Ireland. And the way they've been able to do it is by reversing the hierarchy that situates English as the ultimate; like, in schools, instead of streaming based on English and maths, like we do, they stream based on Welsh, so it gives an advantage to those kids who speak Welsh at home. At least, that's what this Welsh girl was telling me when I was there.'

He looks both horrified and confused, and I recall that only five minutes earlier he had proclaimed brazenly that Asian migrants should only speak English. What identity crisis spiral have I sent him into by suggesting that the tongue in his native land isn't even English? Maybe he didn't even know that the Welsh language existed? He's just proudly brandished his Welshness his whole life, thinking it was just a subsect of ye olde England, used it to crush cultural differences, in determined bigotry, ignorance and hypocrisy.

'Have you heard Welsh before?'

His no is angry and disgusted, and I think it's judicious to move forward into the other stage of the booking. I take his cock in my hands and compliment it. It's not a lie; it is a nice cock. It's just unfortunate that it's attached to such a not-nice man. We move to the bed and as I put a condom on him, slather myself in lube and he begins to fuck me, I have that always surprising moment of oh, I could come. Could come with this guy who I am repulsed by and don't respect and actually already kind of hate and wouldn't notice on the street and wouldn't talk to at a party. One thing I have learnt with this job is that sexual attraction does not equal sexual compatibility, and my body often betrays my sensibilities. We go into doggy so I can avoid looking at him and think of who I really want to be fucking me, and my mind dissolves and I speak in tongues as I always do, truncated sentences of unfinished thoughts, a cacophony of oh my gods and fucks and baby that feels so good I'm going to come.

I orgasm, and we both sit up for a breather.

'You've got a real potty mouth on you,' he says.

And I'm revolted with myself. Wish I could take the orgasm back. Not because he gave it to me — he didn't; he just happened to be in the right place at the right time, I could've come on a carrot — but because he doesn't deserve to think that he gave it to me. The buzzer goes, thank god, because I can't even pretend to be polite to him, and I strip the bed as he showers.

Back in the girls' room I lie back on the couch beneath the *NO SLEEPING IF YOU SLEEP ON SHIFT YOU WILL BE FIRED YOU'RE HERE TO WORK* sign. The Cambodian woman is in a booking that's extended and it's that time of the afternoon between lunch and knocking off work that tends to be pretty quiet, so it looks like I'll be settled in here for a bit. Still eight hours to go. I go to stalk their social media profile again and then force myself to hide my phone under a cushion that I then sit on because it's night-time where they are and it's not like there'll be any new activity since I last checked. I'm increasingly frustrated with myself.

What am I doing?! I don't even want to date them yet I'm behaving as if I do, returning again and again to their profile in the same way I compulsively tear strips of skin from my cuticles. I am one to crush, and crush hard. Often the other person swells in my mind till they fill every crevice, an amorphous shape that becomes a comforting thought to shelter and self-soothe in, a sure thrill when bored. On long drives, in waiting rooms, while massaging a client I can think of them. A place to rest my whirring head. A place of harmless fantasy and fun. But there are not-so-healthy habits associated with this. The need to always be stimulated, to have someone to obsess over, the constant checking of their social media for an illicit endorphin rush, seeking a sign of them thinking of me.

In relationships, all this energy is channelled into caring for my partner – but outside of a relationship I entertain myself with a never-ending daisy chain of crushes to fritter away my time and excess emotion. They pass through my hands as markers of moments in my life, almost indistinguishable from each other but valuable to me for the holding. I like my mind to be crowded with furniture, not empty with echoing footsteps. And a living person is the most convenient occupying force to house there – it really takes up space. What disturbs me is that I don't even want to be with some of these people, yet I still expend energy on their Instagram profiles, stumble down the same paths I follow when I'm actually into someone but without the motivating desire or curiosity. The crushes aren't the problem, then, they're just the excuse I use to exercise these behaviours. Why? What for? Do I not know how to live without a needlepoint of obsession to spin myself around? Must I always be chasing adrenaline? Why can't I just chill — without a drink or a joint or a mindless scrolling of someone's feed?

I don't like myself when I'm into someone. My personality and joy are diminished, my insecurities fester and my boundaries are swamped. As much as I critique the ideas of monogamy and love, I still felt they were a structure I could grow my life on, till it flourished, triumphant, in a wisteria burst of colour and wonder. In a relationship, though, I will sacrifice my mental health for the preservation of 'us' at all costs; I lose myself in my partner. Why am I like this? I prefer my thoughts to be a neat row of securely stabled horses which I can walk among, patting their rumps in satisfaction of the splendid order. I like to know what I am doing and where I am heading and have a sense of surety down into my very marrow. But when I am into someone I lose myself in contemplation, let fancies wash over me and pull me out with the tide till I am adrift in all I do. And when I bob clear I realise not that the person isn't great, but that they shone partly with my own spangling of them. My feelings tinge every aspect of my life; when I smoke a joint my fingers come away pink-stained. I love wholly, completely and unrealistically, and feed the love with the sweet treacle of my own romantic soul – only to realise yet again that it is unsustainable. What a folly!

I curl my feet in the consciousness of my mind; toes caught upon a crush, pebbled thoughts like grit that never quite leaves. I take things – that glance, this text – and play them till the colour fades, till I can take them up and sew them into the narrative of romance that I have strung above my bed, to look at and muse over when I should be asleep. Standalone moments of no importance, but in that galaxy of emotion and hope they take on another meaning. Queer girl writing her own romances, appropriating femme friendliness into a wider whole of wishful wanting, a perfect knit for all weather. A knit to overheat in, a hairshirt to sweat out anxious thoughts of *Does she? Doesn't she? How many million ways can this be read and can I possibly be reading them all wrong?* As women we're raised to take tepid two-steps, to doubt, to let the other make the move. And when you are caught with another girl in that dance . . . How many times have I stepped the same steps, trodden the same tired grooves of my mind, an ouroboros of extreme elation and suffocating uncertainty? How does one get out of this labyrinth? Burn all your romantic novels, cough on the fumes till you spit out the sediment? Bury your pink lingerie in a bed of rock, quell those femme yearnings, become stone? I need to be done with romance in the same way I was done with drinking – because it isn't good for me.

The intercom buzzes at me: an intro. Thank you, God, for the money and the distraction! You really do care about the smallest sparrow, and I need to be kept from my phone.

The client's around thirty and I can tell within a few minutes of being in the room with him that he has an intellectual disability. He's tentative, asking what he can touch and what he can't, and pats my head gently as I suck him off. Dido is playing over the sound system – whoever heard of Dido at a brothel? – and I'm transported back to my single renaissance in Europe; where I played 'Thank You' on repeat out of gratefulness to the world for existing and for me existing within it.

We try doggy but he keeps laying his full weight on my back and it's hard for me to maintain a sexy position beneath that so I get on top. With me in cowgirl, though, he keeps covering his face, peeking through his fingers to watch me ride him. I figure he's shy so I don't say anything (I've had guys fuck me with their eyes tightly closed, or even with their head turned away, as if we're a couple in a fight – I'm never sure if it's a denial of what their body is doing or an escape into it).

'Do you like me being on top or do you want to do something different?' I want to make sure this is okay.

His hands are still over his face. 'Yes. I'm so sorry I'm not good-looking,' he says, voice muffled beneath his palms.

'Wait – is that why you're covering your face?'

'Yes. I'm so sorry I'm not good-looking.'

'That doesn't matter! What matters is being respectful and hygienic and considerate, and you are all of those things.'

He still won't uncover his face, though, and keeps repeating his apology, and my heart breaks a little. I think of all the clients who have treated me terribly and how none of them has ever apologised for their behaviour, and also all the seedy guys who haven't washed under their foreskin yet expect my arsehole to be pristine and ready for a finger at any moment, who want me to suck their stinky sweaty balls with no thought for my comfort, and here is this guy, who has been nothing but kind, apologising for something he can't help but which someone has obviously made him feel bad about before.

After he comes I shower then dress beside him slowly, contemplating the vast divide between my bookings. People are obsessed with what's *real* and *unreal* about my work, as if it can be neatly categorised. Like anyone in any customer service job, my work is partly about treating everyone with the same level of friendliness and respect, regardless of whether we would actually get along outside of that interaction. With some clients I fake orgasm but leave the booking grinning because we are so well matched in conversation. With others our talk is stilted and I'm surprised how quickly I come. Some guys I am attracted to but we are completely out of rhythm with each other. Some shipwreck themselves on the rocks of my anatomy. Others I hope I never see again.

People always ask if I enjoy the sex I have with clients or if I have to fake it, as if the two are mutually exclusive and the interplay between them isn't much more complex. In actuality, it depends. And I'm not sure what people are threatened by more — that I don't always love it, or that I don't always hate it. That sometimes I go into a booking horny, wanting a girl I'm into, and put the guy in doggy so I can imagine it's her fucking me till I come. That sometimes I pretend a yawn is an orgasm moan and count the money I'm going to get over and over as they thrust. That sometimes my skin crawls and I pray for it to end. That sometimes I am filled with hope about the world and humanity as I connect with a stranger I never would've met otherwise. Just because I wouldn't do it if I wasn't paid doesn't mean I don't ever enjoy it or have genuine moments of human connection. Just because part of my work is feigning doesn't mean it's all a sham. Social interactions within a workplace are far more intricate than a simplified *real* versus *unreal*; my job, like many jobs, may be part performance but it's not *only* performance.

I kiss him on the cheek, let him out and wish him nothing but good for the rest of his days, and am back in the girls' room in no time, ankles crossed over the arm of the lounge as I count the condoms in my condom bag, ensuring I've got enough for whatever size dicks lope, drooping heavy with pre-cum, through the brothel doors. In the same way other girls open purses and tampons fall out, so happens with hookers and condoms. They're stuffed into the sides of my car door, in between the pages of books. I pull them out of my pockets when I'm scrounging around for some bud. Multicoloured and branded sheaths of latex, existing in hope and promising safety. In some places sex workers are arrested for having them; just carrying them is seen as proof of soliciting, intention to prostitute. I'm so institutionalised that a condom being put on is part of the foreplay for me: I get wet when I see one rolled down a strap-on, can't even think of a blow job in my private life without one. Sex and condoms go hand in hand, or dick in orifice, flesh or otherwise.

High heels and fishnets are the stock images you always see of sex workers, but for me it's condoms, coconut oil, hand sanitiser and burner phones. It's a truth universally acknowledged that the longer you're a whore the more burner phones you have, and mine pile high in my living room, chunks of plastic that I can't bring myself to throw out in case I need to cross-reference a client's number, or in case I need to switch to a different advertising bracket in private work. Sometimes I start in shock when one rings at a restaurant table and I don't recognise the ringtone. 'Whose phone is that?' I ask, only for someone to say: 'It's coming from your bag.' Oh, right, one of my other identities. It's hard to keep track. Gotta remember to refer to myself as the right name in the right context; gotta switch between calling a close friend Ruby at a friend's birthday party and Lucia when I eat her out in a hotel room and Mimi when we pass each other in the hallway of a brothel that'll fire us if they know we work independently too. No wonder so many sex workers and managers just revert to the blanket 'babe'. One slip-up and you can ruin someone's life, as fatal as a slip-off from a stealther. It's high stakes in hookerdom, but only because society makes it so.

When I have a week off work because of thrush, with no money coming in and desperate to be well again, I'm reminded that I'm like an athlete, relying on my body being working fit. When I squat at a man's groin that stinks of stale urine, grateful for the latex separating his genitals from my mouth, I'm reminded that I'm like a nurse, paid to be intimate with bodies in ways I don't want to be. When I struggle to keep my pose and moan as a client drops his entire weight onto my back in doggy, and I position myself to seem as if I'm backing on to his cock while protecting my low slung cervix from a bruising, I'm reminded that I'm like a performer, hazarding strain to my body while creating an aesthetic visual. When I listen to a man cry about his life, because it's less stigmatised and emasculating for him to see a prostitute than a psych, I'm reminded that I'm like a therapist. When I smile instead of cringe at something a client says, I'm reminded that I'm like someone in customer service, there to respond politely, not to assert my own beliefs. When I coddle a drunken man at midnight, fetching him water and helping him dress, I'm reminded that I'm like a babysitter. When I soothe a bickering couple, manage to make them forget their friction and enjoy something together, I'm reminded that I'm like a diplomat or hostess, all tact and solicitousness. When I handle a fractious man, get him to relax and come and guide him gently into conversation, I'm reminded that I'm like an actor doing the hardest improvisation ever, responding to unconscious cues and crafting a finished product, an experience. When I wash cum off my fingers, which had curved protectively over my cunt to shield it from the spray as I feigned masturbating while a client jerked off over me, I'm reminded that my work is quite similar to so many things, but not quite any of them, and it doesn't need a euphemism. I am just a whore and I'm okay with that.

And I'm a whore who's about to make more money, as the doorbell rings a few times in quick succession, the punch of an impatient man with a hard-on hammering; hammer me, mate. The buzzer rings, it's an intro, and I'm off down the hallway. Damn my arse looks good – if I've ever had enough and the manager is forcing me to intro still, I walk out of the intro backwards so they don't see my best asset and pick me, and by enough I mean the enough when you're fucking your eleventh client of the day and you bite yourself hard on the arm as he fucks you so you can feel and focus on something other than his dick pumping in and out of what feels like the very centre of you – and he's a moustachioed man with leathery skin who obviously thinks he's pretty suave.

He picks me and while he showers I take off my bodysuit, as I always do so we can get into it, but also because I just prefer being naked and sometimes that high G-string rubbing on my swollen pussy irritates it and gives me thrush, so I'll hang around the girls' room with my cunt out, airing it.

As he's drying himself, he says – with a pout that is possibly meant to be endearing but makes me want to slap him – 'Ohhh, you unwrapped the lolly!'

'What lolly?'

'I mean you; you undressed yourself. I like to unwrap my treat.'

I want to remind him that unlike a lolly I can unwrap myself and also can hear and feel and am not to be consumed; instead, I try to pass off a grimace as a flirty smile. He doesn't seem deterred and comes towards me as if intending to seduce me when, mate, I am a sure thing, no seduction needed; must we role-play as if I'm not a hooker?

He lies me down and begins to lap at my nipples in a way that men obviously think is sexy but I am always revolted by – so much tongue that now if I ever hear a dog sucking on a bone the noises set me off with shivers; greedy, needy mouths suckling at me, pretending it's for my pleasure when really it's for their own.

He is French. Some of my worst clients have been French and Italian, I think because they have fallen for this cultural stereotype of themselves as passionate lovers, and so they perform the part with an audacity and smarminess that makes my vagina do a rushed crab crawl back inside myself, knit its lips together and pray for no entry. They always want to make you come, and are confident they'll be able to. Sometimes I delight in telling them that, actually,

I orgasm easiest with clients I'm disgusted by coz I don't give a fuck and relax into it, and then see their confusion when they don't know whether they should pursue their goal or if it would be more of an achievement to make me too nervous to orgasm.

'What's that? Oh, I actually already came today and I can't usually come again so soon.'

If he hadn't already irritated me I would've just faked it, but he can have the truth. Sometimes I err on the unprofessional, break that performer's wall, invite in the blunt Aries me that simmers just beneath the surface etiquette; she's no pushover.

'Where's the fun in it for me, then?' he asks. 'Next time I need to be your first client of the day.'

I bite the pillow so she doesn't snap back, gotta keep that tongue on a leash. I just wish he would leash his tongue, too; I can feel it slobbering in my ear canal.

And my mind is off, thinking about them while he fucks me, the worst possible thing to be thinking of because with every move of his I'm aware it's not them. It feels sacrilegious to have his hands upon me, a travesty. I want to cut them off at the wrist, could hang them from the ceiling, an art installation to go among the classic brothel art, dismembered body parts casting shadows on the pastel nudes and yonic oils. If I owned a brothel I would make sure there were no more weird colonial rooms, the exotic and oriental among the pop culture, Karma Sutra Room, Hollywood Room, Jungle Room, Morocco Room, James Bond Room, no tribal statues or Asian fusion. There would just be the petrified penises of ugly mugs tacked to the board in the office, instead of CCTV screenshots. *There's* a blacklist that'll actually stop them hurting a woman again – and oh, hello, he's getting harder and faster, my cervix is braced in protest but I won't stop him coz he's so close; just tickle his balls and grit your teeth, girl, and there we go!

He lies back panting and I lie beside him for one brief minute, say that was nice and stroke his chest because I can afford to be affectionate now that he's finished. I don't dislike him as much when there's nothing left to dread. Then I spring up to shower, can see from the clock that time's almost up, and I've got less than five hours to go and I've got that adrenaline from money making, want to eat through all the men like a silverfish through a pack of cards, leave them in chewed disarray while I'm plump on the proceeds, twitching my cute little antennae at other working girls.

I let him out and I've got a booking waiting already. Scoff a slice of pizza, pat my puss dry and I'm back under the same portrait I fucked under earlier today, odalisque side-eyeing me in solidarity. *Live! Nude! Girls!* signs on strip clubs proclaim, but *Live Nude, Girl* is what she says to me in pride and bemusement. *I did it too and here I lie for eternity; sold my body and it's lived beyond me, stretched into the future well after I decomposed, just as you live on in the memory palaces that clients craft around you, as they say, 'Let me have one last look at you before you cover up, for my spank bank later – you've got the perfect pussy.'*

'You've got the perfect pussy,' this new client says to me, predictably, and I think of the collective subconscious and how there's no greater proof of it than the patterns of a sex work establishment. The troughs and peaks of the industry that every working girl tries to rationalise, but really there is no explanation as to why men – like beaching whales – come in herds, turgid members filling our hands till we are overworked and then they leave us, barren and needy for money, for days at a time. Why one night every girl goes home with a green-lined wallet, and the next you are all frantic with stress as the night extends long and quiet with no doorbell ringing to shatter the slab of time, rising ominous and money-empty ahead of you. Girls become superstitious. Oh, I always make money in this set, last time I made bank I had this necklace on and now I have to wear it forever, it's windy today and men always come when it's windy, the feng shui is off I better wash each stone from the water fountain stone by desperate stone in the kitchen sink, if I start eating they will come, last Monday was busy I better roster on for next Monday. Tearing out your hair to make a pattern of it; sending yourself crazy trying to predict which shift will cover your rent. Uncertainty drives you wild.

And I'm driving him wild. He's hallooing and howling as he gets closer to orgasm, flopping like a fish and giving tongue like he's chasing something sweet inside me. Tally-ho, I want to cry, what a ride! Horse girls are the best roots, didn't you know? *Puberty Blues* says so and so does my arse in reverse cowgirl.

Wipe up his cum, shower while he gets his breath back, strip the bed while he showers and I'm waiting with heels and condom bag in hand while he ties his shoelaces and off we go down the hallway; damn, I'm efficient – got him happy and out of here in under half an hour. My pussy's a lubed-up portal that twists time. How many men have time travelled through it today, how many men will travel through it in my lifetime? In this moment I can take them all.

And I'm back in the girls' room and without even thinking I'm back on their Instagram. Jesus fucking Christ why can't I curb myself like I curb a 500-kilogram racehorse, with firmness and finesse? Does my mind need an even tougher hand than my own? This is stupid and this is it, the last time. No more wallowing in those waters of fantasy – you want escape, read a book; no need to be the protagonist in a love story. No more filling the space she once filled with them; be single in thoughts, not just action, and let your mind soar. No more falling back into the same complete preoccupation that you have in romantic relationships. No more no more, a crow croak of wisdom.

'Hey, honey, how is your day?'

She's got gloves on now, preserving her moisturised hands post booking. We've all got our little rhythms and routines. I'll smear my cunt with Canesten as a thrush preventative when I go to sleep and only send voice notes to friends so my wrist can recover. Physical labour takes its toll.

'It's been good, busy, and none of the clients have been too bad, so I'm happy.' I want to add, But I can't stop thinking about this person in Europe and it's driving me crazy – not so much the thought of them but the fact that I have so little impulse control my mind just drifts back there inevitably like tyres on the gravel corners of a country road when you're tired and each time you come to with a start and wonder what the fuck you're doing there and whoa that was close I almost crashed or almost sent them something stupid really, if we're no longer talking about the figurative – but saying all that would just be giving into my desire to speak about them and chew over them in conversation like a cow with cud grinding molars and pap and also she doesn't need to hear that mundane shit so instead I say, 'How about yours?'

'Good, honey. That client, he extend three hours and he very easy, just want talk-talk and kiss.'

I offer her some pizza but she's got her own food, and then just as I think of watching something on Stan the doorbell rings. We both intro and the guy is obviously drunk and oh god I hope he won't pick me but he probably will coz he's that fit middle-aged white-guy type who always does, sees himself reflected in me, Aussie on Aussie.

I'm right, and we spend the first ten minutes of the booking arguing about complimentary drinks because he thinks he should be entitled to two free beers if he's booking me for an hour. The receptionist ends up coming to speak to him herself because he won't take my no — that I've received from her through the intercom — as an answer. Keep arguing, mate; you're just using up the time I'm being paid for.

Now he's lecturing me on investments — as if I've asked for advice and have money to invest — and speaking about his extensive property portfolio, which I always find a bit tactless. Cool, you make money flipping houses, and I have to suck your dick to have a stable rental. I fill my mouth with it now so I don't voice my frustration and disdain, and surprisingly he gets hard within the condom. I go to get on top and this guy won't shut up.

'The GDP, which stands for the gross —'

'Domestic product, I know.'

Oh god, I shouldn't have said that. He's taken it as interest rather than a correction of his assumption of my ignorance. He repositions my body onto the side and as he enters me he continues, 'So the four big players are China, Russia, Germany and the United States,' and he's punctuating every country with a slow, deep thrust. What am I meant to do in this moment? Am I meant to be learning or enjoying? Can I settle on a halfway moan that expresses both curiosity and pleasure? Is this what my life is, an audience and receptacle for dull men? It's not so bad really; after this I'll go to bed in one of the work rooms and then I'll wake up and fuck on the bed I've just dreamt in, not just one man but a few, and I'll do that week in and week out and sure, that's drudgery, but think of next month when you go home for the long weekend and then think of next year when you go overseas for a month and then think of next decade when you might finally be able to afford a house, something that he sees as just a property but you'll see as a home, and that will last forever while he's just one link in a chain that you're heaving yourself along, giving you callused hands that your future children can hold in love and pride and that your current friends hold in trust and adoration, because friendships are the real romances in life, the enduring till death do us part, and any crush only offers a poor shadow of what you get from your friends already, that's why you'll spit that

European from your mind with the same force that you're spitting on his cock now – yes, come on my tits, that's hot. My life reaches beyond this moment and beyond this obsession and beyond this man.

tuesday

I'M LIKE, 'GUYS, CAN I PUT HIM DOWN YET? HE'S ACTUALLY really heavy,' and I keep crying with laughter and swallowing my hair in the wind and I'm worried about climate change but right now I'm not anxious coz I'm here with you all in my favourite place in the world, but please don't mention the one billion native wildlife dead coz I just want to forget about it all for a few hours or half a day maybe, and yeah, we're a world embarrassment coz we've voted in climate change deniers who will do nothing about our horrible rate of carbon emissions even though we are gonna be one of the first countries directly impacted by climate change and I even feel conflicted about having children when the world will probably end but also isn't having children an act of hope and surely if all the people who care about the world stop having kids out of conscience it's just gonna mean the next generation is even less populated with people raised to fight for this earth and, 'Have you got the shot yet, guys? My arms are really starting to ache!'

And the pup's down and off to touch noses with the cows through the fence, cows that surely felt the fear just like I did in the weeks when the fires crackled around here, destroying Orara, terrorising Coffs and touching the very edges of Dorrigo rainforest. Gondwana, my soul cried, day in and day out, those forests are not meant to burn! Thousands of years they've been safe in their lianas and wetness, and now, because of us, they sputter and smoke. For two months it's been black in my heart. I've gone to work, I've gone out, I've distracted myself. I've donated to anything and everything to combat my futility. But the future feels bleak and I feel powerless to change any of it.

For weeks I've woken up repeatedly in the night thinking the house is on fire, then I realise it's the bushfire smoke in the air. It makes me cough, makes my throat hurt, not surprising since being outside in Sydney most days has been the equivalent of smoking four to ten cigarettes. As the fires have swept along the east coast – not just burning eucalyptus forest

that is regenerated through fire but desecrating rainforest that has always been too wet to burn – I've
been constantly anxious. For once, though, it's a
rational anxiety. It's hard not to panic when family
members are evacuated again and again, when fire
draws close to your home, is put out, starts up again.
You mourn and hope and hope and mourn. You sit
in your backyard and a friend asks what's falling
on your face. 'It's ash.' You run into someone who
survived Wytaliba, and they tell you of the hundreds
of skinks scorched dead on the ground after the
fire went through, an entire ecosystem turned to
crisps. News reports list the hectares burnt (18.6
million), the houses destroyed, the human lives lost.
Besides the koalas, though, the animals go unmentioned. Internationally only UNESCO seems to
acknowledge that this is a tragedy on a global scale.
And the forest is simply 'hectares', not the loss of
each individual tree. The government denies and
diverts, and you feel suffocated. You are suffocated.
Your house is on fire.

Now I'm back in my home area, in this untouched
valley, and the wraparound mountains of the Great
Dividing Range hide any fire damage from view.
We're cocooned here and could almost pretend it's
over, or that it never happened, except that we know

from the news that it's now the South Coast that is being pummelled, beaten into submission just as the places I hold dear were weeks ago. Hernani and Lowanna and Ebor aren't only names on a map to me; they are places I love and sobbed over. And the world is waking up to it. The images coming out of Mallacoota, apocalyptic scenes of people marooned on beaches, have caught the world's sympathy in a way that the nonstop bushfires from September to December didn't. The apathy hurt me almost more than anything. For months my home was burning, and it felt like no one cared. The only overseas friends who checked in on me were Australians, and yet every morning I woke with tears and donned a mask inside my own home, because it wasn't airtight and the smoke infiltrated everything. Is it because we're in the Southern Hemisphere that we can be so easily ignored? (Is this what the people of West Papua, Sudan and Palestine feel constantly – overlooked?) Do people from other countries assume it's the norm for Australia to have bushfires and so they don't notice our pain?

Not like this, though. It's not meant to be like this. It's meant to be controlled burning, as First Nations people have practised for thousands of years, tending to the earth. Colonialism has choked that with its greedy paws, through genocide and displacement and eugenics, and our government does not heed the voices of those who have survived, those who should be listened to most intently. The land is parched, too, from drought and overuse, bled dry by cotton and mining and selfishness.

How does one wake with the strength to live another day, to fight, when everything feels utterly hopeless and you feel helpless to change any of it? I know I need more than resilience, I need fortitude, and I know if everyone who is exhausted gives up then we're done for, and there are people so much more exhausted than me, who have devoted their entire lives to causes, yet every morning I wake heavy with doom. And unlike friends in other parts of Australia or the world who can disconnect from it, have moments of self-care where they don't go on social media or read the news, in Sydney we've been unable to escape it for months because in the very air we breathe there is a constant toxic reminder that we can choke on and even see, so tangible it obscures the end of your street and even the sun. And our prime minister, who belongs to a church that believes in the end of the world and divine providence, a church that started in the bible belt of Sydney and has now been exported to LA's elite, goes away on holidays because to him maybe the continent burning isn't a terrible foreshadowing; it's all part of God's plan. I will never forgive him for this, and I hope the Australian people never forget it.

Stop thinking about it all. I'm back home now and the sky is clear. I'll never take clear sky for granted again. I know my dad was that way after the bushfires of 1994 wrecked the Upper Hunter. It's why he relocated us from Wollombi to Bellingen, because he never wanted to live through fires like that again. I was a baby and so didn't understand, but now the fear and the dread has entered my psyche too. And now, less than thirty years later, the fires have followed him north, to the place he thought would never burn because it always flooded. How wrong he was! How wrong we all were. The audacity, the arrogance, the ego of humans to think we could reap what we liked from the earth with no consequences.

'What's that? Yeah, let's have a joint – I'm tripping too hard to roll it myself, though.'

My fingers are mottled and stumpy and my foot pulses from that bull ant's bite as we trudge back through the grass, stepping over logs and dodging thistles. I'm looking down because the view is too overwhelming. So much green and blue that it comes screaming in at us, 360 degrees of eucalyptus and us, just one irrelevant pinpoint squished by those techni-colour surrounds. As I light up on the verandah, I'm reminded that the world is best viewed from between a horse's ears or down the length of a joint. The land rolls off in one continuation from my hand, down to the mandarin trees along the creek where the cows hoover the dropped fruit up whole, *shloooop*, across that one unsightly blotch of state forest that reminds you of so many awful things better not thought of now so don't think of them, up to the smudge of the ocean twenty kilometres away. And off to either side, into the great beyond and beauty that I am a part of.

'I'm having a moment, guys,' I say over my drag.

Looking around, we are all lost in our own moments. What feelings of grief and horror in their bodies, I wonder, are temporarily soothed by the tranquillity of nature? I know none of us has forgotten what's going on. On the drive up we stopped to pee among the charred remains of eucalyptus forests that had been home to koalas; kilometres and kilometres of burnt trees alongside the highway, empty of birds and the sounds of life, black and brown and grey where there used to be green and green and green. We pulled over in silence, gazed at the ravaged planet in silence, drove on in silence. What could be said that we didn't already feel and know? That we have destroyed this earth, the only earth we know, which we should have treasured above all things.

We – the general we, the human race, but more specifically the non-Indigenous Australian we – are culpable for what has happened to this continent. And then I, the white Australian me, who loves this country like no other, whose biggest heartbreak was losing the property she grew up on, whose night-mares are of the red cedars being chopped down and lantana overrunning the riverbanks, yet who is able to be in and love this country only because of the dispossession of the Gumbaynggirr. How do I reconcile myself to that? Maybe it's not something that can be reconciled.

'What's that hanging off the trellis?' she asks as she reaches for the joint I'm holding out to her, breaking my contemplation.

'It's a snakeskin.'

'Did you put it there for decoration?'

'Nah, the diamond python just conveniently rubbed its shedding skin off there.'

'The diamond python?'

'Yeah, the one that lives in the roof. It lives off all the rats there. They're harmless, don't worry – non-venomous.'

'Is that the main snake you get around here?'

'Yeah, that and red-bellied black snakes. We don't get many brown snakes, which is good coz they're quite aggressive. Red-bellies are venomous but they're pretty shy; they won't hurt you if you don't bother them.'

'What does a red-bellied black snake look like?'

'Black . . . with a red belly.'

Everyone laughs and because of the acid none of us can stop; it goes on in waves as one person stops for breath and the others start up again, witches' cackles that leave our cheeks aching and gums dry, to the point we're laughing at our own laughter, the absurdity of ourselves and of being together. My belly starts to cramp because I'm laughing so hard, and it's so much better than the empty sickness of anxiety that I've felt for months, that has had me hysterical in the girls' room at work on days when the wind blew towards my home and the Fires Near Me app sent me constant notifications and clients asked me how I was and I would say, I'm okay, I just can't stop thinking about the fires, can you? It's just so terrifying and awful and there's nothing I can do, and then they'd shut me up by putting their dick in my mouth and then I'd fuck them with such force in reverse cowgirl that I could continue to read the updates between their legs without them noticing, one hand teasing their balls while the other flicked the screen. Panic that became panic attack and then numbness and then back to panic and all that's coming out now in this purge of a laugh that I've needed more than anything.

'Anyone wanna go lie in the bath to break the heat?'

A gay guy friend and I squirm naked into the cracked enamel tub, outdoors like true Australians, and one of the girls plucks sprigs of rosemary and chucks them in with us as the bath fills with cold water, so we feel like lamb being basted on a high summer day, thirty-three degrees at 4 p.m. The night'll be long and close with clouds of insects but at least I'll smell sweet – not that there's anyone to get close enough to smell me. This is the first New Year's I've spent single in five years; that feels like a significant thought but I don't know why. Will I feel sad? Weird? Lonely?

'Hubble bubble toil and trouble,' the girl says as she stirs the rosemary into the water around us, encouraging the two of us to flop around the bath.

'We should add rosemary to the punch,' suggests my friend in the tub. 'It smells so nice.'

'We should just make more punch in here, then we'll have enough for days,' she says all gleeful, as if moved by genius.

'I'm getting out before anyone decides to pour the champers in here; I'm not just a non-drinker, I don't even like alcohol on my skin — so sticky.' And I clamber out of the tub as people are squatting on beaches down south watching towers of smoke pour from their vanishing family homes.

Climate change anxiety it's supposedly called. The way my mind circles back to that same point again and again. Just when I think it's moving forward it veers off, and no matter which way it loops it ends up back there.

The pup comes running up, a little staffy with his cow print and pink nose, a gift to my friend from an infatuated backyard breeder at a gay club. (That's the kind of thing that happens when you're strikingly beautiful.) He's puffing in the heat and so I throw him into the bath with the sprigs of rosemary and the squiggly black things — 'Wait, what are they?'

'They're my Mauritian hairs, babe — I'm always moulting.'

'Filthy gorgeous,' I say, and he rubs his brown pecs in response.

Once the puppy's damp through to the skin we take him out and roll him dry in the two-day-old hay left by the mower. He nips with needle teeth, oversized paws akimbo.

'Wish I could be rolled by hands bigger than my body in a haystack. How nice would that be?' I lie down in the grass to illustrate my point. Wish I could gather all my friends together too, have them all in this pocket of the world, sprinkled out from my pockets where I carry them with me always, watch them bloom and grow, revel in the joy they find in each other. 'It's thriving, doll,' said one of my gay guy friends about that break-up vine that is climbing the wall of my living room, leaping from mantelpiece to painting to picture rail, a literal metaphor of my progress post relationship, and that's how I want to see all my friends: thriving.

They're scattered all over the world, though, and try as I might I'll never be able to hold them all at once, a bouquet in my arms. They're in my heart and mind, though, and sometimes I recite their names like a chant in my head to ward off sadness. There's been a lot written on the chosen families of queers, how being rejected by their biological family often leads queers to seek out and form connections outside it. I don't know if it is my queerness that has made me this way, but for me the blood of the covenant is thicker than the water of the womb. And 'friend' is a hallowed term in my mind, one I value more highly than 'family'.

'So are you a relationship anarchist then?' a girl at the dog park asked me once.

'Well, no, I wouldn't say I was, because while I'm anti the hierarchy imposed by the state – you know: valuing familial and sexual relationships above all others – I wouldn't say I was anti-hierarchical in general. My friends definitely come first. But maybe that's reactionary . . . maybe if the state didn't place so much emphasis on the others I wouldn't feel I had to place so much emphasis on friendships; they could all be equal. Also, I'm too much of an emotional monogamist when it comes to romance to really practise relationship anarchy.'

As I said that her dog started humping my leg. She shooed him off, saying, 'You're a little poly dog, just like your mother!'

It was an interaction possible only in the inner west of Sydney; up here the dog would've got a smack on the nose and a 'Get out of it!' Up here you wouldn't even be at a dog park, unless you lived in town. They run out their energy in the paddocks and sleep outside on the verandah, as all dirty dogs should. What's an Australian country home without a wraparound verandah and a few kelpie–collie crosses barking at the end of a chain or coming out from under the house, shaking dust off their coats and scattering chooks who'd been bathing in a shaft of sun? Growing up here we went to parties in muddy strips between dairy farms, pumped music from car speakers, stepped over the carcass of a cow while sculling goon. Up here I got bullied at thirteen for being an 'ugly lesbian', and then when I came out at fifteen and my body started being seen as desirable to the same boys who had ruthlessly taunted me in my younger years, who started trying to pull me into cars at doofs, I was demeaned as a 'fake lesbian slut'. Sure, suddenly I was of interest, but my identity was still something that I couldn't assert, was theirs to define. I think of friends of mine who grew up in Sydney's inner suburbs and went to expensive progressive schools, where there were gay couples in year seven and they had 'wear it purple' days to celebrate diversity, and how so many of them sleep with who they want and don't define themselves as anything, saying, 'I'm just me – I don't need a label.' And I wonder if they are blasé about labels because they were always accepted, whereas being gay at school in Coffs Harbour was not okay, and was in fact very weird, and I couldn't wait to get to the big metropolis one day where there would be more people like me, where I would no longer be an outsider, and my concept of myself developed around my sexuality because my sexuality was seen as an issue, a topic, coz no one's parents or teachers were gay. People would come up to me as we stood around the bonfire and say, 'Are you that lesbo? So how do lesbians have sex?' Then I'd make out with some other drunken girls and show my tits for half a can of Bundy and laugh as some town kid slipped in the mud and grabbed onto an electric fence for support.

My flawed home that I'll allow no one but myself or another local to criticise! When a New Yorker makes a dig at it, compares it to the confederate South, my pussy dries up in protest, drier than the rocks in the riverbed in a drought, when the water goes underground and the eels clamber across to another swimming hole, the same sleek eels that twist around my legs when I skinny dip at night. In the background I hear Thelma Plum sing about her hometown, and I think about Thora and how I want to be a voice raised for it and from it. How often do we read over and over again about the same cities of the world, see the same streets again and again on the big screen? I want to see the latticed sky of stars, the Milky Way aglow, that hangs above a country road as you stumble home, ferns silvered with dust. I want the figs and the jacarandas and the blackbutts, and I want the story of how I ended up, labia stretched and plush, on an oil-slick bed — because, sure, men like Henry Miller have written excessively about whores, but to them we're just a slit between legs incapable of valuable thought or real emotion. I want you to know that you may be able to squint up inside me and count the men I have slept with, like rings in a tree, a tracing of lines that coil up and through me till I'm pricked like the tallowwoods beneath which the cows graze, yet none of them have erased where I'm from or who I am.

'What album is this?' a friend asks and I'm drawn back into the now. The peak of the acid has definitely passed.

'*Better In Blak*. Thelma Plum — she's a Kamilaroi woman.'

'Kamilaroi?'

'You know, they're Aboriginal people whose lands are inland northern New South Wales and southern Queensland. The Kid Laroi is one too; that's where his name comes from.'

As I say that Thelma Plum references the 1967 census in her song and I think of how only then were Aboriginal Australians recognised as people, not flora or fauna, and how colonisers attempted to eradicate them from these arable lands and how even the name of the great river that all the others feed into, the Bellinger, is corrupted from the native name. A typo on a map, a white man's mistake that changed an *n* to an *r* and no one cared coz they didn't care for the people, so why would they worry about the language? Didn't care for the country, either, and thus it burns now. Don't think of it don't think of it. Think of the cool of the Never Never River that winds its way past you now. It's not the Rosewood River, the one you grew up beside, but they have the same sweet source and reach the sea at the same point and the same clouds shatter above them till they burst their banks at the same time and feed the valleys that feed you.

'Should we go look for shrooms? There might be some down in that hollow past the creek where the sun can't shrivel them up.'

Five of us wander down the hillside, crawl under a barbed-wire fence and slosh through a cattle wade. The creek is cool against my ankles, shaded by rain-forest palms, and I take a small rock to suck the river water from, hold it in my mouth even after the sweet-ness has gone because it's so smooth. We begin to scour the paddock as the cows creep closer, curious.

'What do I look for? Are these white ones all right?' A friend holds up a mushroom as big as her fist.

I garble an unintelligible answer before I remember to spit the rock out and try again. 'Nah, not those. The ones we want have, like, a gold top, and if you split the stem when you've picked it there's a faint blue tinge.'

'I've never done this kind before, only blue meanies and that was so long ago, with Katie. Why didn't she come by the way?'

'She wasn't up to being in a group at the moment – and also her parents wouldn't let her come. They thought it would be too much for her and too much for us to take her on in the state she's in since she relapsed.'

'Oh, is she using heroin again?'

'No – which is good, I guess, but I don't know if this is any better: she's messing with Tina now.'

'Tina?'

'Sweetie, you're showing your straightness,' another friend chimes in, teasing. 'Tina is ice.'

'You know I'm not straight – I'm just not that up with pop culture.' She shrugs. 'I thought *RuPaul's*

Drag Race was a show about cars up till a few months ago.'

'Nothing to be ashamed of,' I say. 'And leave her alone, you know she's practically a boomer! Anyway, yeah, Katie's been on the pipe and her behaviour has been pretty erratic, even scary. Like, she ended up having a psychotic break. I've been super worried for her and I was hoping that coming and chilling with us for a few days would be nice for her – like, remind her that she has a normal life outside of rehab and NA – but we gotta respect her parents' decision.'

'Also, maybe it isn't the best thing for her to be around us when we're taking drugs?' he suggests.

'Yeah, true. I guess I thought because we aren't dabbling in things that are an issue for her – like we don't have coke or xannies or heroin or meth – it'd be okay. But I think that's coming from my own relationship with drugs: I can touch things I don't have problems with and I'm fine, like, as long as I avoid alcohol and uppers I'm all right coz I can control myself with the things I take. But I guess what I'm beginning to realise is I can't view her addiction through the lens of my own. Like, maybe she's one of those addicts who have to stay fully sober for the rest of their life and need the structure that NA gives them, because with her it's like if she has a drink she'll want a xannie and then she'll want to smoke meth, like they're all tied together somehow.'

'Do you reckon that comes from NA, though? Like, they put so much shame into people over being "clean" and "relapsing" that if they touch anything at all they feel like they've failed and may as well go the whole hog.'

'Yeah, I do wonder if it's counterproductive to link recovery to shame, but then maybe some people need that hard-line approach to keep them in check. Maybe shame is one of the few things controlling them. But, yeah, I don't think it's a particularly healthy outlook.'

'It's so sad for her and her family,' she says. 'Do you reckon she'll be able to stay sober?'

'Look, I don't know.' I shrug. 'I think that maybe this struggle with addiction will last her whole life, and I need to stop being so invested and upset when she slips up coz it's inevitable, it's not going to be a straight road. And she said something to me the other day that made me think of it differently. She said, *I wish my mental health problem wasn't addiction*, and I was like, fuck, true, she is grappling with such a different beast from me because, like, I just struggled with substance use as a way to self-medicate through times of bad mental health but she's – oh, yay, here's one!'

I pluck it out and hold it up and they both crowd around to look. 'Where are the others? They need to see, too – oh, they're over trying to take photos with the cows . . . Oi, guys, come over here and see this so you know what you're looking for.'

'That's so hectic about Katie.' She puts her hand on my arm and I rest my head on her shoulder in response, encircle her waist with my arms as we wait for the others, lean into the affection offered, shroom held like a cigarette between index and middle finger.

'Yeah, it sucks. Also she did and said some pretty fucked things this time around, and it's like at what point do you hold someone accountable and at what point do you just forgive coz they were obviously unwell?'

She turns and kisses me on the forehead and I remember that five years ago we used to make out and I wonder should we make out again tonight because it's New Year's and maybe it's meant to have been her all along but no, we have such a beautiful friendship, look at where it's come to when it started with a simple flirtation, and it's fine to have moments of being attracted to your friends, it doesn't mean you need to act on it, you can just appreciate that it's there and will always be between you and doesn't even need to be acknowledged and so I just give her a slight squeeze and lean a little more until –

'If you lean any more weight on me I'm gonna fall over!'

'Oh, let me be lazy, hold me up,' I kid, but I step away.

'What's that over there?' one of the others calls, sounding startled.

It's a goanna, long-clawed with fetid breath, clambering slowly over a log, tongue flicking the air. 'Give him a wide berth,' I say. 'Goannas'll chase you and climb you like a tree, tear up your flesh.'

He's come down out of the rainforest, fleeing the fires up on the mountain. There've been more pademelons hopping through the paddocks than I've ever seen before; they usually stick to the thick brush. And usually you only see the wild dog/dingo hybrids on their forays to slaughter the calves. Now it's a menagerie, an exodus, the area crawling with displaced animals just as it does in flood time. In flood time bullrouts are washed downriver to the shallows, where they stab you with their poison spines. Flood time may wash some unwitting dairy cows out to sea, their bloated carcasses polluting the surf, but the platypuses are prepared for it, their burrows built above the rising water levels. They all know about flood time, but what do they know of fire time? This forest isn't meant to burn, not like this. I've seen photos of parrots, their feathered bodies of red and blue and pink and green, dead on the ground, choked by the fumes even as they tried to fly away, just as koalas curled in the tops of trees fell and burnt when the smoke became too thick. The genocide never finished here; colonialism still kills and now it's part of a wider mass extinction.

Do they know we did this? Do they hate us? Don't think of it. There's nothing I can do to stop it right now. There's maybe nothing I can do to stop it ever. The power lies in the corporations that drain the country and the politicians who are ambivalent towards anything except profit. It's a new year beginning and what a cursed beginning it is, the last months of 2019 marked by skies better suited to dystopic sci-fi films than the world I want to wake up in. I'm here with my friends, though, think of that. My home is still safe. I'm not bound by a romantic relationship. These are all things to be grateful for.

The sun drops behind the hill as we trample back up to the house, pull sheepskins out onto the verandah so we can lie on them and lean into our comedown, fern fronds tickling our ankles that dangle off the deck. My head is on the lap of one friend and another friend is using my thighs for a cushion. A drink is poured and a drink is spilt and a joint is rolled and a joint is smoked, and this seems to repeat itself endlessly, like the call and response of the whipbirds on the fire trail, our voices sighing and creaking in laughter like the branches of the blackbutts in the wind, our bodies entwined like the structures the satin bowerbirds weave in an attempt to draw a mate and propagate, so the next generation will live on in the same privet hedges and banksia bushes they did, and isn't that what we want too, for our next generation to live on as we have? I know I want my children to be able to whale watch, sip honeysuckle from its source and be pierced by coloured coral. More than that, though, I want the earth to survive us; would trade all of humankind for the earth in a heartbeat. God doesn't barter, though. Does the devil? Please, hear my prayer.

wednesday

THE TARMAC JARS MY SHINS AS I STRIDE PAST THE ART gallery and a couple of brush turkeys scatter into the mulch. These shoes aren't made for fast walking, they're heeled and impractical, and the white cockatoos on the fence of the botanical gardens jeer at me as they throw down shredded fruit. I know, I know, I'd be better off barefoot like you guys are, but I've got a booking to get to and I can't show up with my soles black from the city pavements. I'm budget enough as it is; gotta make sure I always park far enough away from the job that the client doesn't see my old car, which would ruin the illusion of me being a high-class escort worth $600 an hour. I can get away with a bare face and nails because I market myself as a wholesome girl next door, come straight from a swim not a shopping spree, but the fact I get around by bus or a dodgy 90s car doesn't need to be disclosed. Let them think I Uber it or, even better, taxi it and pay with $50 notes like I did when I was twenty and did a brief stint at an escort agency. The smell of Chloé still takes me back to 5 a.m. in the back of a cab, streetlights glancing in the windows and mascara grit in my eyes, rolling out of bed only to fall asleep in my Gender Studies lectures, double life concealed beneath my floral dresses.

That was before I knew anything about the industry, didn't know I didn't have to give a fifty per cent cut to a management that pressured me into doing things I didn't want to do. Sent me out in taxis across the city, each residence a gaping maw that might never spit me out again. The danger fit my idea of what sex work must be and I thought what I was doing was illegal so didn't think to wonder if I could work more safely or deserved better treatment. Seven years later I know better: I work in brothels or for myself, and I've given up those gruelling nights. So here I am, striding through the city at 9.50 a.m., a morning delivery to a guy with morning wood, and I don't have to split the cash with anyone.

I'll meet him in the lobby and, unlike that first time, I won't be self-conscious, don't care that the scarlet letter emblazoned on my soul shines brightly.

Don't care that I'm in the elevator with a man thirty years my senior. *So what*, my hair flick and upright shoulders exclaim, *I'm a working girl*. Judge me not lest thou be judged. I've got the hardened shellac exterior of a pro now; the prostitute, the professional, from whom judgement slides like water off a duck's back. The way I make my living is no better or worse than anyone else in this grimy scramble to survive (that's what the clack of a working girl's shoes sound out on the parquetry, if you've ever wondered). I've become bold, almost brazen, and here I am under this beautiful blue sky and isn't it a blessing to be alive!

It's also my day. These passers-by may not realise when they walk past me, but if they keep walking to Boy Charlton Pool they'll see all the gays with their chiselled, oiled abs out. They've flown in from all over the world because guess what? It's Mardi Gras, and the city is ours for two weeks. Obelisk and Redleaf become beats beneath the sun. I'm close to the Cross now, too, which the government has tried to kill with lockout laws and gentrification. Strip joints closed, clubs replaced with yuppie restaurants . . . No queue outside World Bar now; Oxford Street is a ghost town. Only ARQ and Bodyline beat a faint pulse of what once was, and the casino keeps the score, shows the corruption in its teeming crowd. It's still ours, though! You may think it's deserted, yours to roam, but really it's haunted by the gays of years past, spectres of the AIDS epidemic that roost by day in the top floor of the Bookshop Darlinghurst and by night come out and plague the straights. You may think these streets are yours to walk, but they belonged to someone else before: the queers, the hobos, the junkies, the trannies, the prozzies – these streets were theirs before they were yours so be careful, you may find you have to wipe your shoes clean before going into your nice apartment. Don't forget, when you stand under the refurbished Coke sign, that those who were despised and reviled formed these streets, literally. No left turns up William Street was simply a way to deter clients from picking up a sex worker, by making it harder to turn their cars around to go back when they saw one who tickled their fancy and their balls. The first supervised injecting room, Les Girls and Tilly Devine – all here. When I get an STI test at Kirketon Road Centre – *Health For All* – and walk to a booking at Springfield Avenue, where I'll screw a man in a co-ho's apartment and dance back down Victoria Street high on money, I think of all the other whores who've done the same and how, even if they've destroyed the red light district, as long as there are still some of us working here there's still a red light blinking, and just like the drag queens bashing a homophobe in Taylor Square and the twinks sniffing amyl in Universal (the Midnight Shift reincarnated), we're honouring the history and keeping the Cross alive: they haven't murdered us yet.

Though we do get murdered. Not necessarily because of who we are intrinsically from birth but because our deaths are less likely to be investigated by authorities because we are seen to be worth less than other respectable women, expendable: not an innocent victim but a woman who has invited such treatment through the very nature of her work. We're the favoured targets of serial killers; Jack the Ripper, the Green River Killer and any other violent perpetrator who has benefited from the acronym NHI ('no human involved') being assigned to their victims, an acronym that has been used by police for those deemed undesirable – black people, homeless people and sex workers among them. And God help you if you're someone who is devalued from birth already and takes on our profession, like a black trans woman sex worker, because society certainly won't! I feel a little kick of fear in my belly now, as I always do on the way to a private booking, even though I've screened the client, because it's private workers who tend to get singled out and every date I go on is a blind date. The brothel I'm at has been so slow lately, though, since this new coronavirus thing, because it employs a lot of Chinese migrant women and racist idiots assume that they're more likely to carry it, even though none of them are recently returned from China and it seems that just as many of our cases have come from the United States. So I'm grateful for this horny man, whoever he is; I'll just lay my hand on this paperbark tree momentarily as I pass it in the hope that he's all right; touching living wood rather than dead brings better luck.

I'm passing through the clipped grass of the Domain now, which always gives me joy because of the way it came about. Originally created as a private park for the rich by Governor Macquarie, it had a high wall around it that the poor kept breaking down and climbing over so they could get drunk and fuck inside. The wall kept getting raised and the poor kept getting in and being rowdy, till eventually the barrier was demolished and the park was given over to the people as a public domain. It gives me hope that more spaces can become public spaces; all those reserves of the rich, such as golf courses and private gardens, should become accessible to everyone regardless of wealth or postcode – it would help to justify the water they guzzle. My favourite thing about the United Kingdom is that the public's right to access paths that have been used for hundreds of years trumps private ownership. I wish that existed everywhere. Privacy is a right, sure, but not when it gets to the point of hoarding – sorry, Madonna.

I enter the lobby right on time, and the client is a generic private client. White, middle-aged, suit. I surreptitiously text the number of the hotel room to my housemate as I walk through the door with him, making small talk, and then comment on what a good view he has, as if I haven't seen the view of Hyde Park from every hotel room in the city already. He wants to chat to me a bit first and he's pretentious as fuck, wants to parade how intelligent he is and size me up at the same time. Says something about my tan and asks how I cultivate it; I answer honestly that I don't try but I swim in the ocean most days so inevitably I'm tanned.

'Did you know that tans only came into fashion in the 1900s?'

'Yeah.' Of course I know that; it says in my ad I have a history degree. He probably thinks that's just copy talk, though. The worst thing about rich clients is they're always surprised when you're smart, as if it's shocking to have an articulate person doing physical labour. My working-class clients usually treat me more like an equal and aren't shocked that I'm intelligent, whereas my rich clients always have this condescending attitude, like 'how lucky are you to be around me and exposed to culture by me'. I guess if you're working class you know jobs aren't necessarily a summation of your abilities, you do what you need to do to get by, but if you're upper middle class or upper class you're more likely to think your job is a reflection of your innate capacity.

'And do you know who it was that changed the prevailing fashion?'

'Coco Chanel, when she accidentally got sunburnt on holidays and came back with a tan.'

'Wow, you and I are going to get along! I didn't expect someone like you at all.'

There's the backhanded compliment I was waiting for; it always comes.

I ignore it and begin to kiss him, moving my hand down to his fly. Let's get this moving; we can chat afterwards, if there's time. Play with his cock, let him eat me out for a bit, move into 69 and put a condom on as he mauls my clit and I try not to jerk away, squeeze some lube on without him noticing, jump on in cowgirl, go reverse cowgirl for a bit, move to missionary and kiss him with feigned passion then hold him tight against me as if I want all of him inside me when really I just want to rest my head on his shoulder and think about other things, enthusiastically suggest doggy and he blows in that after a few minutes like they almost always do. I love when everything goes to plan. Now we can chat away.

'You know, you're so interesting to talk to, I would love to just meet up to pick your brain – we don't need to do this other stuff.'

'Yeah, we can do that for sure. I do offer social dates at a lower rate.'

'Oh no, I didn't mean that – I respect you too much for it to be mercenary. I feel like we could be friends; don't you feel that?'

He respects me so much that he can't respect that me spending time with him, regardless of what we do in that time, is work to me?! How do you wrap your head around that, Mr Penthouse Suite? Why do the richest cunts always want shit for free!

'Yeah, I do feel that, but this is my job. It's not just sexual labour that I do, it's also emotional and intellectual and I have to be reimbursed for that. It doesn't mean I don't like you, but if I saw every client I liked for free I wouldn't be able to pay my rent.'

'I just struggle with the transactional nature, though. I feel it adds a performative element to it, and you're so interesting you don't need to be treated like a prostitute, and I don't like feeling like a john.'

'I don't think of any of my clients as johns; it's not a term I relate to. That's used more by people who want to denigrate and homogenise clients, when I think there's nothing intrinsically wrong with paying for sexual and emotional intimacy – it's a basic human need.'

'Yes, but you understand what I'm saying: I view you as more than that. I respect you as a person, I don't see you as an object.'

Wow, I wish he did just see me as an object, because at least the guys who want a blow and go, as if I'm a pocket pussy, don't try to wriggle out of paying me!

He's now going into an absurd justification of wanting to spend time with me for free which I zone out of, but my ears prick up at a mention of Marlon Brando – how did *he* get dragged into this?

'. . . said that we're all partly acting in life, so he refused his Academy Award on the basis that he couldn't accept an award for acting when we all act in our day to day.' This guy scatters references like signposts proclaiming how cultured he is.

'I thought he refused his Academy Award because of the treatment of Native Americans in the film industry,' I say.

'Well, yes, that too,' he admits reluctantly.

It seems we're at an impasse. I can see by the bedside clock that there's only five minutes left, thank god, so I excuse myself to go shower and get the hell out of here. He talks to me while I do, making a few derogatory comments about brothel workers and how he would never go to one because they're not of the same calibre as me. Wish he could've seen me on my knees in one two nights ago, giving a gobby to a cock that had already been inside me, all for $90, and coming up with a rash on my legs from the mouldy carpet. Mate, the only difference between a brothel worker and me is marketing. We're quite literally the same person.

As I kiss him goodbye he invites me on an (unpaid) trip to his Paris apartment, when he's next over there from his home in New York. ('A girl like you needs to be taken to Paris – you're too good for here.')

I wait till the door closes before I roll my eyes. Babe, I've taken myself to Paris already!

Brush him off: it's easy to do on a day like this when you've got a queer party to get to. I strut back

141

through the city and a lizard with a long striped tail winding down the sandstone wall watches me with his yellow eye as I kick off my shoes and start to skip along the pavement. He's immobile and I'm jittery with excitement, but we're both triumphant and soaking up the sun and I blow him a kiss and wish him a good day. I'm $600 richer and my feet are bare and life is good – what more could a girl want?

I guess there are other things I want. I want to have a stable home that I own so I don't have to worry about where my dad will live now that he's nearing seventy with no money and no assets. I want to speak another language. I want to have children. Beyond that, though, there is nothing I want that I don't already have. Sometimes I'm almost startled by my own lack of ambition. I have no great desire to be someone, prove myself, achieve things. As long as I have the respect of those whom I respect and continue to work on myself, that's enough for me. I feel content. I feel loved. I feel grateful. I feel ready to be a mother. Should I want more from life than friendship and financial security, though? Shouldn't I be wanting to make my mark on the world? Isn't that what your twenties are meant to be about? Does it make me parochial not to have 'big' dreams? Or is the

idea of success and happiness being caught up with

career and social status limiting in itself? We value ambition so much that my lack of it makes me wonder if something's wrong with me. I do have big dreams, but they are for the world, not myself. I want more for the people in it and I want the planet to survive us.

Kylie comes on the radio and excites me out of my reverie. I'm going to see so many friends in such a short time! Don't need no uppers when you've got that Mardi Gras adrenaline running through you; the spirit from those people who marched in 1978 and got arrested and beaten by the cops charges the whole city, and not just the city – it spreads outwards through the suburbs, pulsing in the hearts of queers. Even straight people feel the vibe and want to be a part of it, and corporations want to cash in on that pink dollar so that you've got a No Pride in Detention float alongside a Liberal Party float. Remember, it started as a protest and it's more than a party, I want to say to the apolitical people who come along for the glitter and glam. Remember that there's still a wealth disparity between queer men and queer women; remember that trans women are getting murdered; remember that there are gay asylum seekers locked up in detention right now; remember that lesbians can't get our IVF subsidised by the government, unlike heterosexual couples, because we're 'socially infertile' not 'medically infertile'. Remember.

I pull up in front of mine and the balcony is already bustling. I've got friends up from Melbourne and they're sorting out their outfits, there're bare bums and bags being tied up in condoms and shoved into nature's pockets and temporary tattoos and one lone friend smoking a durry and regaling my cat in Tagalog. A 'Late Nite Tuff Guy' remix of Kate Bush is playing and I leap up the stairs, skidding on eucalyptus leaves as I go. 'Guys, guys, guys, that client was such a dick! I'm just going to have another quick shower and then I'll be ready!' Ready to have a bump, ready to drape myself over people in a Marrickville gutter, ready to have epiphanies on the dance floor, ready to live. My last few Mardi Gras I was deeply depressed, but now I'm back inside myself. I'm not just a shell going through the motions; I'm overflowing and giving back to those around me: come have some of my joy, I've got enough to share, you can see it peeking out the tip of my stripper heels, wedged in between my toes, sparkling at the diamante crotch of my bodysuit, in the bend of my back as I pose for this pre-party shot. I'm all me and all confidence, none of that blight of anxiety that riddles my brain till it's moth-eaten and stunted.

Now we're piling confusedly into two Ubers, the vinyl seats sticky on my bare arse, hope I don't leave a dollop of ovulation, have I got my ID?

'It's taped inside your hat,' one friend answers, which is a relief, especially when I didn't even realise I asked that question aloud.

We're here and I'm tottering out of the back of the car, tripping over the tree roots, popping a quick squat and having a quick snort of K before going into the venue. We're on a suburban street, but it's a suburban street that's used to the loudness and nudity of the 'el-gee-bee-tee-eye' — I recite the letters as I stamp my shoes on the pavement in impatience. 'Hurry up, guys, I wanna go inside!' Now I'm singing the letters to the tune of the nursery song 'Farmer in the Dell' — will someone please think of the children? Not the hypothetical children that conservatives claim to defend, but the very real children loved by all these queer parents here today; the children who have been raised by a village just as I hope to raise my children, surrounded by those I love.

There's an older gay man on the door and that's one of the things I love about Sydney, how intergenerational the queer scene is — this party itself has been running since the 90s, and there are dykes here with the eyebrow piercings they got back then too, chapped and capable hands that I'd quite like to feel rough against me, to hear them say, Your skin is so smooth, like they always do, and I say, Thanks, you can go inside me if you want, you don't have to be careful with me, I'll only say 'gentle' with my eyes rolled back to temper your enthusiasm when you're a fist deep, otherwise I'm yours to touch as you will.

I've been touched a lot lately by lots of different hands, not just clients'. I have finally worked out how to have fun casual sex in my private life without investing or inventing emotionally. I always believed it was possible in theory, though not necessarily in execution. The last few months, though, I've blithely gone from bed to bed, watched a trans guy shakka in satisfaction after I orgasmed on his strap-on, so huge that he had to ease it inside me with two hands. Let a non-binary person fuck me natural, their clit swollen from T damp inside me, rubbed wet against my arsehole like the teasing of a sea anemone. Repositioned myself on a client's cock so I could feel my bruised cervix, like tonguing a pulpy gum, sweet reminder of an even sweeter fuck with a girl in Brisbane, eyelashes curling up at me as she ate me out, mouth below water level like the snouts of the crocodiles rumoured to be in the drains beneath that city. All of them I'd fuck again, none of them do I have a desire to date, and I don't stress about how they feel about me. I've been honest about my intentions; I'm not toying with them for validation, I just want to be one of their toys every now and again – but unlike the toys stored under their bed I don't stay the night, I just come (to their house, and in their bed) and go (home, with wetness cold and uncomfortable in my underwear afterwards). I want to be touched with lust and kindness, and touch back with gratitude and respect, don't need them to message me or interact with me online, it is what it is, mutually beneficial, bend me over your bedpost and we'll meet in a moment of unabashed need, forget about me after till your clit knocks against your boxers and you know it's time to text again.

I'll probably see a few of them here today, not that I'm down for it now, I just want to dance and be ecstatic and have nonsensical conversations with people while we slap sunscreen on each other's backs; you've got to remember that hole in the ozone layer, partying responsibly isn't just about carrying naloxone or keeping your tummy full. We're dancing under some shade cloth outside and there's a trans boy I know jostling around at my elbow; I should introduce him to the others.

'Guys, this is Louie.'

'Oh, we know each other! We met in Berlin, right? And Melbourne before that? But I think you had a different name then.'

He nods. 'Oh yeah, Melbourne, that was three names ago.'

'Queers, I can't keep up with the whole move cities, change name thing. I've just got my work name and my real name.' I am teasing or maybe I'm flirting; flirting with this fine day with the blue up above and the colours I'm immersed in, the other partygoers parakeets of rainbows and chatter.

'Yeah, but you're cis. It's more of a gender non-conforming thing.'

True, I say in my mind or from my mouth, not sure which, but before I can determine it the moment has passed and an Egyptian woman with curly hair has put on a house track that makes the crowd collectively drop down into it, knees braced and souls singing. We get deep. You can feel the shared ecstasy; it shimmers above us, a mirage of heat and euphoria rising from all our bodies, trapped between the shade cloth and the sky. There is no place in the world I'd rather be. Actually, I think I am in the best place in the world right now, in this exact moment, I – There's someone touching my hip. I glance down and it's a friend of mine in a wheelchair, someone I wanted to fuck till I found out we were both bottoms.

'Oh my god, hey! Wanna dance with us?'

'I'm about to head home; it's getting too crowded, not enough space for me to turn. I came earlier when the dance floor was empty. Now no one looks down and they keep tripping over me. It's going to be a struggle getting out . . .'

'Want me to clear the way for you? I'm taller than most people in these heels.'

'Yeah that'd be great,' they say, and so I strut through the crowd asking people to make room so they can pass through and think about how I take my body and my ability to move through the world for granted, how this venue is accessible but even then they have to leave once the party really gets going, and how I've never been able to invite them over because I live in an old terrace with a spindly staircase, and how later tonight I'm going to go to a club that they'd have no way of getting into.

I kiss them goodbye and as I go to head back inside to the party a woman crashes into me, and

it's the Lebanese lesbian who used to be the receptionist at a dodgy brothel I worked at. She was the
best to work under because the clients all thought
she was a man and so were on their best behaviour,
but all us girls knew she was a woman and so felt
comfortable with her in the girls' room. Really, all
brothel receptionists should be butches of some kind,
I decide. And multilingual ones, too, I resolve as I
remember her berating a difficult client in Arabic
and him apologising profusely in a way I would never
have been able to get him to.

'It's so good to see you! Wanna come to the bathroom with me?' I gesture at my nose so she knows
it's my shout.

'Yallah, let's go!'

On the way we grab a Tongan trans girl we both
know and the three of us cram into a toilet cubicle.
My hands are sweaty and so I gush eagerly as I
repeatedly fail to roll the note – 'It's so good to see
you it's been way too long how are all the girls is
Vanessa still there and what about Sharni and Lexi'
– and she's answering all my questions and then the
Tongan girl takes the note from me and says, 'Let
me do that' so I give myself over completely to the
catch-up conversation.

'Oh, I wanted to thank you for getting that girl to take down that photo by the way,' she says to me.

'Don't worry about it. I'm still outraged she put it up.'

'What happened?' the Tongan girl asks as she delicately sniffs up a bump.

'Wow, you do that so elegantly! My nose sounds like a rusty tap.' I take the note from her and explain, 'Well, this chick at work, white queer girl, took a photo of her on shift at the brothel without asking and then posted it on Insta without asking. So fucked. Like, the first rule of a brothel is you don't take photos of other people – and then to post it online?! And the worst part is she captioned it: *This is what a brothel looks like.*'

'Nah, the worst part is that we'd just been talking and I'd said how my migrant identity eclipses my queer identity and how I don't relate to a lot of white queers and then, I guess coz I'm obviously a POC and obviously queer, she decided to post a photo of me to destigmatise brothels or whatever, which I get, but it used me as an object and was completely at my expense. And imagine if my mum had somehow seen that – yi!'

'Yeah, like, using you as a tool in her own political agenda without considering the risk to you? Makes everything she says about community care and stuff like that pretty hollow.'

'Babe, that's fucked – did you call her out on it?'

'Nah. Maddy just messaged her for me asking her to take it down. I didn't have the energy to explain to her why what she did was fucked; waste of my time if she didn't already know how wrong it was. I just hope she isn't endangering other people's privacy like that. She can't just waltz through life thinking everyone can be as open about working in the sex industry as she is.'

'Who's Maddy?'

'I'm Maddy; she just called me my work name by accident. Violently outing me!' I playfully flick her.

'Fuck, I'm so sorry.'

'It's all g, I don't care. Just do yours already and let's get out of here. I wanna dance!'

We go back out and the dance floor is heaving, and I know that I have a wonderful life and a wonderful future ahead of me, and a camp gay I know looks me up and down and exclaims, 'Bodyyyy!' and I feel powerful within it because I know it's brought me so much. I was just a country girl who moved to the big city with nothing but my body, earned it all ten toes down and legs up, hamstrings strained and tight from horseriding, no familial connections or money, climbed that ladder one dick rung at a time, the ka-chiiiing of my pussy its own kind of art, just as valid as the art pumped out by middle-class kids with a family home and inheritance waiting.

I think of all the men who have beached themselves, sperm whales, upon the crest of this arse, defeated in doggy, lying exhausted and prone and sapped of their virility, gently lapped by my blonde beach waves in their post-orgasm comedown, my pubic hair seaweed-slick to rest their head upon, their fingers pruned from reaching to get back to the waters of the womb from whence they came; did they want to climb inside me? I wonder. Tuck themselves up behind that same shelf of bone that I struggle to extricate my sponges from? Hollow me out till I'm nothing but a domestic chamber to play house with (in)? Do they want to swallow me or be swallowed by me?

Three thousand and counting, grains of sand that have burnished and furnished my golden life, forgettable as individuals but meaningful in their multitudes. I think of the person that I sent this arse to as a booty call years ago, someone I should've kept as a friend and a fuck but I skinned and pulled taut on posts and stretched them into a (pleather) partner, tanned and tended them because it's what we both wanted. I think of this arse pushed up against someone who can fill me right up, between our rape play and lingerie. Sex worker/writer/mother. Who says thoughts of pregnancy have to be untarnished, somehow chaste even in the midst of a sexual act, thinking only of that greater act, missionary and medical? Thoughts of pregnancy get me on all fours, wanting and dripping. What better climate to create in?

It's all play because everyone I want to fuck can't actually creampie me, though I gag on their strapon more than a flesh and failing dick, and beg them to take me raw. Maybe that's why it makes me so hot for it: because it's all just womb-aching and not womb-making. My child will be conceived with careful planning, its own kind of love more stable than romance, a different kind of fairytale. I'll spin my hair into gold and turn tricks with this arse, flip them over till they're guppy-mouthed, gasping for breath as I wipe up their mess, like a baby having its nappy changed, infantilised.

And someone is spanking my arse now, and I turn around to find a beautiful redhead friend of mine who has already said yes to giving me his sperm, how serendipitous, just when I'm thinking of my children-to-be, surrounded by my family-to-be, here's my donor-to-be right up against me. Not that he's the one and only; I have a few more gay friends who've said yes, and then there's also that straight friend of mine in Sweden who I want to ask. I'll say to him, Hey, I know your lifestyle doesn't work for having kids, but if it's something that interests you in a non-traditional way, like being a distant dad with me as the primary carer, I feel like we could make it work coz I know there's mutual respect and trust and we're both quite pragmatic and responsible. I would happily sign a contract so you know I'm not after financial support in any way, and you appeal to me because I know you wouldn't be up in my business wanting to be with me, you're smart and diligent and, most important of all, treat women well, and you could knock me up just by fucking me, it's a lot cheaper and more statistically successful that way. Damn, I'm into fine-tweaking this pitch – can't wait to actually deliver it!

'What are your brands?' someone next to me asks, and I must've been carrying on a conversation while my imagination was off frolicking in my future, and so I say, 'I'm not really into brands.'

'No, I mean what are your pronouns?'

'Oh, right, lol, sorry – she/her. You want to get up on the platform with me?'

From the vantage point of these seven-inch heels I can see over most people's heads but I want even more, I want that change of perspective, want to see the undulations of the crowd beneath me, be the observer and the observed, feel the might of a height I never normally have in this petite body, with my clothes and personality always bigger than me. I want my physical presence to match the strength I feel within, want to be carried up high with elation, float like a balloon above this day that I love, these people I feel close to even if I don't know them.

The person next to me hands me up to a babe with sharp acrylics and I wouldn't mind being tied to their apron strings, hope they don't let go of my hand, I don't want to drift away on the breeze, astral projection a distinct possibility if I keep smashing that ketamine; pace yourself, girl. My phone buzzes in my hand and 'Superstylin'' begins to play and I open the text to find that a friend who has been going through a rough time, barely staying afloat through addiction and mental health issues and financial struggle, has texted me and something else has gone wrong for them, I don't know why they are so jinxed, life keeps knocking them over, won't cut them any slack, and here am I in my jubilation and my wonderful life that I hold in my hands and shake with excitement like a dog worries a ragdoll, all grip and boisterousness, and I wonder how can I be having this most marvellous moment while my friend is suffering, and I can feel that I'm crying silently because there's nothing I can do to help them and I just want them to be as rich in their life and future as I am.

'Are you okay?!' the babe next to me asks.

'Yeah, sorry, I'm actually great, but I just got a text from a friend who is going through a bad time and I feel so sad – I just wish I could give them a slice of my life or what I'm feeling right now because life hasn't been fair to them and really I have so much, I am so happy.'

The tears are streaming down my cheeks and I don't bother wiping them away because it's a testament to my friend that I feel this sorrow, because they deserve more from life. So many of us do. I have at points, and now I'm finally milking it, and here I am drunk on an excess that I never thought I'd have, filled myself straight from the teat of the divine, let it froth on my lips, and now I wish I could churn it into cream to share with all my friends, till they were all fed and satisfied with the smug smile of a cat. That's not how life works, though; sometimes we can only care for the people we love, not fix things for them. And everything isn't meted out as it should be.

Three Aboriginal drag queens perform as the sun goes down and people are beginning to move inside to where Ayebatonye is finishing her set or heading to various kick-ons scattered across the city or chilling in the gutter talking about what next, but not me, I've got another club calling me, and this one's dank and claustrophobic, down some steps and through a tight corridor with poor ventilation and clogged toilets, where everyone smokes in the bathrooms and gender is irrelevant and you sweat out all the toxins you've consumed as if it's one mass sauna because that one broken fan never works and it's thirty degrees if not more in there, your clothes sliding off you till you're in nothing but underwear, drenching the tarmac with sweat when you go out to the street for a life-saving breather. If today was light and goodness, tonight is promiscuity and a smear of caked white scum across your face, refuse from your nose that's stuffed from one too many lines. The side of the queer community that people want to clean up, brush off, put in a suit so you can get a rental, cram into a beige turtleneck and shove a glass of champagne into your hand, talk about the art we make that straight people buy.

I don't want that, though. I want to keep the dirty, the glory holes, love seeing a girl peeing into a sink because the cubicles are all taken by orgies or rack fiends; I've been that girl peeing into the sink.

'Why are they dressed like prostitutes?' a straight guy who had never been to a queer club once asked my friend. 'Well,' my friend answered, 'it's a queer club, but a lot of them *are* prostitutes.' That's because there's a huge crossover between working-class queers and sex work, I barely know one who hasn't dabbled in it. The flow between black queer culture, trans culture and sex worker culture is vibrant and unending. Our clubs are full of whores. To pretend otherwise is to pretend that the economic disparities don't exist, to pretend that I don't sell a lesbian fantasy to my clients, capitalising on and contributing to the continued fetishisation of Sapphic relationships to fund my lesbian reality. Here I am now in my high femme garb, knowing I can move through the world as a middle-class person, know I am afforded that by my whiteness and tertiary education, knowing that I wouldn't have the latter without sex work, which allowed me to transcend my welfare years and drop the references to travel and culture that other people get through their parents' wealth. Here I am, dancing to Honey Dijon in a basement in Woolloomooloo, hemmed in by other bodies that have hustled like mine and hearts that have felt and minds that have rankled and wombs that have bled tears of melancholy and tits of silicone that glow in the dark and cat eyes that are smudged from fingers that have grasped a face with lewdness and tenderness, and there's a white lesbian with age crinkled around her temples tugging at my bodysuit wanting to ask me something, and I bend down to hear her say, 'Are you one of those girls . . .'

'Am I one of those girls?'

'Are you one of those girls that are just here for the night . . .'

'Yeah, I'm here for tonight,' I say eagerly.

'Are you one of those girls . . . that are just here for the night . . . that aren't really gay?'

I'm shocked into silence. I'm used to not being seen as queer, to my presence being interrogated because I'm 'straight passing', but on Mardi Gras?! What is with this overemphasis on aesthetics in our community? I understand the need to signal to others through coded dress, but when that excludes those who either don't have the will or don't have the means to access a certain look, where are we? Left with a reading of other people as authentic or inauthentic based on what they wear — what a flimsy way to perceive sexuality! Everything I wear is inherently queer, because I am queer – in the damp of my pussy, in the crook of my elbow, in the sprigs of my veins. Clothes are simply a garnish for this body, not the summation of it!

Whatever, who cares. I'm at the epicentre of the world right now, molten figures all around me, melding in this heat into one amorphous mass of skin and bliss. I look across at one of my friends, who is wearing nothing but sneakers and a loincloth, and I see an expression on his face that I can feel on mine, one beyond words, and I know everything has been worth it to make it to this moment, all paths led here and there is a greater purpose. I feel God in the room, just as I feel God as I gaze over the rolling hills of Dorrigo, and know God is between and with us sometimes when a partner and I make love. Forget the false idols; we should love ourselves and each other like this always, because we are made in God's image, in all our flaws and follies, only human – and, yet, isn't it incredible to have this chance at life? I am so lucky to be alive and to be surrounded by my community, to be held by my community, to be passed from hug to hug with a hey hey hey hey hey let me lean on you for a sec so I don't fall over in these heels.

After this I'm gonna sneak out to smoke a rushed joint with a puff puff pass babe let's smash it so we can get back to this set at 4 a.m. and then I'm gonna contemplate kick-ons at 5 a.m. but go back to mine instead coz there's a bathtub we can lie in while the magpies are carolling and we wait for Woolies to open and at 7 a.m. I'm gonna get a call from someone going baaaabes you still up come to Newtown, and I'm gonna be washing the dirt off my knees and untangling my hair and I'll say no but let's get pho together this week. And I'm gonna open my iCal for the first time in three days and sigh as I remember my responsibilities and see the brothel shifts ahead of me and I'm gonna think about how I'm there for the taking, ripe for the picking, to be had but not in the sense of being a mark, more that I'm not hard to get, all you have to do is pay me, I'm an easy lay, unhindered by virtue, supposedly carrying a high body count as if it's a disease or baggage, when in reality the soul is self-replenishing and limitless, not a finite source that is whittled down to nothing with each conquest and paid request, I'm not the wilted rose society thinks I am, petals picked by all and sundry, I'm louche but not loose, my pussy like any muscle becomes stronger with each use, till it can pull men in and crunch them up and all that's left of them are some crumpled $50 notes. And really the only people I've ever been truly had by are those I've fallen for who haven't liked me back but have bathed in the validation all the same, because that's what they were interested in, not me. I know I could probably be plucked like a fresh flower again in that regard, all naivety and softness — more fool me!

thursday

thursday

'ARE YOU AFRAID OF CATCHING THE VIRUS?' HE ASKS ME AS he dresses post fuck. Funny that they never ask me that beforehand. I guess it might ruin the mood; no one wants blue balls even in the midst of a pandemic. I want to ask him, Are *you*? You've just had direct contact with me, even begged me to kiss you, and I lied and said I had a boyfriend because clients always respect that more than my own boundaries.

'Not really. I've done this work for seven years and the risk of infection is a reality. There are things I'm way more scared of catching than corona.'

My body has always been on the frontline with this, the threat and awareness of illness and violence are occupational hazards. Prudently checking they don't finger me with the same hand they just fiddled with their foreskin with, holding the condom as **167** they pull out so no cum spills inside me, making a snap decision to leave my heels on so I have something to kick them off with if need be because they seem suspect.

'Oh yeah, like AIDS.'

'Well, I mean HIV isn't a death sentence in this country, you can get access to medication, and if you're undetectable you can't pass it on. But, yeah, that would be a big deal for me because it is illegal to do sex work in Australia if you're HIV positive, even if it's undetectable. Plus, it's a chronic health thing you have to manage for life. So yeah . . . I can't afford to take time off work anyway, especially now that brothels are gonna close. I need to make as much as possible to tide me through for who knows how long. And personally I'm more worried about not having enough to live on than corona.'

'I heard it's not really that bad for young and healthy people anyway.'

'Totally. I mean I'm not scared of catching it myself but I am scared of unknowingly passing it on to people, and I feel like especially with the work I do, coming into contact with so many people, it's on me to be as responsible as possible. I actually stopped socialising a few weeks ago, coz I don't wanna be an accidental super spreader. I figure clients know and accept the risk they're taking in coming in here, so I don't feel guilty about that, but I would hate to pass it on to others outside.'

He gulps and looks uncomfortable. What, man, you want me to delude you into thinking you're not taking a risk? You've chosen your horniness over the safety of the wife and kid you mentioned, whereas I'm here because I need to survive, and I'm not going to ease your conscience about that. We're in a pandemic, watching the death toll climb every day in Italy and the UK, and we all need to make sacrifices. I haven't seen any of my friends in weeks and I ache for the company of someone other than a client. Spending every day at the broth, which smells of sperm and bleach as they always do, my skin cracking from soap and hand sanitiser as it always has, knowing that I'll invite repulsion if I contract anything because sex workers are already viewed as carriers of disease, my body already seen as contaminated even when healthy. Knowing that I don't have an employee contract to support me through the brothel closures, knowing I can't work from home, knowing I have no family members in a position to lend me money.

And I've got it good compared with so many! I'll at least be able to apply for Centrelink to cover my rent. So many of the migrant women I work with here can't. The beautiful Vietnamese woman I always sit with (the only girl who regularly chats with me on shift because, like me, she can't speak Mandarin or Indonesian or Japanese, and the girls' room, like prison, is split by language groups; Brazilian girls travel in impenetrable packs in Sydney's biggest brothel) isn't eligible for any government support and says to me forlornly, 'Baby, I'm homeless,' when I ask what her plan is. I've let that sheepish client out and am back beside her in the girls' room and there's a tension that I've never felt here before. None of us knows what's coming. We're all just gonna fuck and fuck and earn and earn and squirrel away as much as we can for the winter ahead. The doors have to shut at midnight tonight, along with pubs and cafes and anything else deemed non-essential. I'm doing a fourteen-hour shift to catch every last penny I can.

'It's okay, though, baby – they say I can stay on here even when it closes. I will be lonely but I am not afraid. At least I am not having to pay rent.'

You can feel the fear, in the 1.5-metre spaces between us and the way we furtively step away from each other in the hallways, the temperature gun that the manager holds up to each client at the door, the distant wave instead of shake of the hand in intros. All the other white girls have vanished; they started to disappear when corona became all too real. To normal jobs, to online work, back to their parents' house. The media is saying that COVID-19 is showing up the inequalities and disparities in the way people live, and I suppose the sex industry is a microcosm of that. Now when the frantic weekend manager commandeers our intros with her sales pitch she goes from, 'Here is Angel, most beautiful Chinese girl, very sweet,' and, 'This is Nicole, busty D-cup, Japanese, so naughty and fun,' to, 'Here is Maddy. Maddy is Aussie. Here till six o' clock only. Aussie. Maddy. Aussie,' because nothing else needs to be said to set me apart.

It's true that it's the selling point for many clients. I wish someone had told me sooner that I could make bank if I left the city and worked in the suburbs with higher migrant populations, where less white girls want to go. Sure, I make less per job. But I'm so much busier that it works in my favour, and it doesn't bother me that I'm being screwed on a dodgy mattress that's straight on the floor; I don't need fancy wallpaper and an open bar to tell me I'm worth something. I know I'm not what these men pay for me. None of us are. Most of my clients are Pakistani, Chinese and Indian, and they almost

171

always say, 'You're the first white girl I've ever been with.' I'm sure, though, it's less conflicting for me making money from being racially fetishised when I don't have to deal with the everyday exhaustion of being reduced to my race in Australia. All of it is in my favour.

This client who has just picked me is no different. 'You're the first white girl I am seeing,' he says in slight awe as I take him to the room. 'Are you from Sydney?'

'Nah, I'm actually from Northern New South Wales. But I've lived here a few years now. What about you?'

'I'm from Myanmar.'

As he showers I fiddle on my phone and my stomach begins to churn as I read the news and see other sex workers panic on Twitter. What are we going to do in these shutdowns? How long will it last? Will sex work become a scapegoat, coronavirus used as an excuse to pass anti–sex work legislation? The water is off, put your phone away, pay attention to him. He hasn't paid to feel your fear, he paid to feel your body, and maybe he just wants to forget everything that is going on for one brief window of the day – you can give him that escapism. Kiss gently down his torso; his skin is smooth, which I'm glad for, no hairs to pull out of my teeth.

'Do you like girls being on top?' I ask him as I squeeze some lube onto the condom, wipe off the excess and put it inside myself.

'I like you any way.' And he reaches out to pull me against him, he wants to feel all of me on him in cowgirl, and he's so soft that I don't mind as much as I usually would. Also, who knows when I'll feel human touch again? Maybe I'll be grateful for this in a few weeks' time, hold the memory to me like he's holding me to him, along with the feeling of that girl lapping at my arsehole in a double yesterday, can't remember her work name but she's so sweet, lent me her fork that time when I was struggling to eat with chopsticks – hope she'll be okay through all this.

We move to missionary and he orgasms almost immediately; we have so much time left that when he pulls me down to lie alongside him I don't resist. We can be post-coital. Besides, I'm feeling almost nostalgic for this work. It's been a part of my life for so long, and sure I hate it at times and get burnt out and never want to be touched by a man again, but now that it's being taken away from me I am senti- mental about these moments of calm, alone with a stranger, while the world is chaos around us. Float along with me on this piece of debris, the brothel bed, symbolic and soulful, don't take your arms from me, who knows where we're headed.

'Has it been a while?'

'Yes. Four years.'

'Four years?! Why so long?' I'm shocked. Often clients will say a few months, they've just got divorced, but more often they say a few weeks.

'I was in Manus for four years — I was only granted asylum a few months ago.'

Manus. The detention centre. Australia's shame among many shames. Where we lock up people fleeing poverty, persecution and certain death. Forget about them because they're conveniently offshore. Who am I kidding, though? We'd probably forget them even if they were interned in the midst of our cities. I don't know what to say. I can't even begin to imagine his last four years. I don't want to go silent on him, though; they pay for interest as well as touch, and I shouldn't let my guilt bind my tongue.

'Did you come with your family?'

'No, with my friend. We are both Rohingya. But he was only kept there for eight months.'

'What? Why? Didn't you have the same asylum claim?'

'Yes we did. We don't know why. The only thing is he is a lot lighter than me.'

Our country doesn't deserve you, I think. And I press closer to him, because all I can give him right now is the warmth and comfort of my body, when we're entering a time in which he'll be deprived of it all over again. Deprived by the state, except this time it's not blatant and unnecessary cruelty.

The buzzer rings – it seems we're going to be deprived by the clock! No more lull to spare, we shower and I let him out and there's four intro rooms filled that I move between, Hey I'm Maddy lovely to meet you Hey I'm Maddy lovely to meet you Hey I'm Maddy lovely to meet you Hey I'm Maddy lovely to meet you, and then I bump into another girl doing the same and we both sputter sorry and step back to make room for the other and then we both step forward and giggle and my eye is caught by the porn playing in the intro rooms, I can glimpse it through a gap in the curtain, and I think of how it primes the men so that they'll come hard and fast and leave happy and we can get to the next booking even faster and I think of how the same tired tapes have played eighteen hours a day, seven days a week for fifteen years and how now those screens will be dark for who knows how long and will the hallways

nothing but my body

miss the girls, I wonder, will the rooms miss the sounds, will the walls miss the touch of a hand in doggy and will the building miss me and the way I run nude through it, garbage bag in hand, after emptying the room bins, discarded desire dragged along behind me? Some people call me a cum dumpster but they're wrong: that goes in the condoms that go in the tissues that go in the bins that go in the garbage bag that I'm taking to the dumpster. I am simply the brothel poltergeist, a noisy spirit. Fuck me, I moan, go deeper, I implore, I'm gonna come, I lie (there), or maybe I don't, I'm no pillow princess, though 'palace' this may be, you can tell from the royal red of the sheets, the classic bordello hue, the same red that I bleed on clients in clots, I'm so sorry, I apologise, it's never happened before, I insist, you're too big for me, I lie, or maybe I don't, maybe I say, Oh no, my period must've just come, as if the head of their dick wasn't pushing a sponge deep inside me, as if I didn't know it was close to overflowing but I hadn't had time to squeeze it out between clients, barely had time to take a rushed menstrual shit and clean my arsehole with soap and water. Is this how whores of the past lived? I wonder. Is this how I'll go back to living, or is this virus the death knell of what I know?

'Maddy, room one. How long are you staying till, by the way?'

'I'll do the whole fourteen hours, till close,' I say as I escort the client to the room I've been using, the same room again and again to avoid cross-contamination in these dire days.

He's a white guy, a minority in this establishment, and we're into it as soon as he steps out of the shower; he's hard before I even touch him. He begs me for a bareback blow job and I act demure and say, 'Sorry, I have a partner, and there are some things I save for my personal life.' He dirty talks throughout, hassles me for kissing, and when I say no kisses all over my cheeks and face, as close as he can get to my lips without actually touching them. I look past his ear and smile wryly at my reflection. It's easier to cope when we're in on this farce together. I'm with her. After he comes and washes himself off he says, 'So you're doing a fourteen-hour shift?'

'Yeah, I am. We have to close at midnight so I want to work as much as I can.' And I step into the shower.

'If you're doing such a long shift you should really have some mouthwash as an extra precaution, to protect you.'

'Well, I don't do kissing or BBBJ, so I don't think that's really necessary. I take the precautions I need for the services I do.'

'I'm just saying it as a doctor.'

'O-kay.' I roll my eyes as I scrub his cum off my tits.

'You also should get tested regularly – you know, STI tests. Bloods, urine etcetera.'

'Why are you assuming I don't?'

'I'm not. I'm just giving you my professional opinion, as a doctor.'

'Dude, you were the one begging me for BBBJ as if it's not risky! And I'm also a professional. I can assure you I know how to be safe in this job.' I flick my towel in frustration.

'Don't get worked up. I just know you wouldn't mix with many medical professionals so I'm giving you some helpful advice.'

'No you're not, you're being condescending! Why is it every time I see a doctor client they lecture me as if they know more than I do?'

'You've seen other doctors here?'

'Yep, many.' And they're always the most annoying, I want to add – superior attitude, think they're the most intelligent person who's ever deigned to set foot in here. Instead I hop on one foot as I shimmy back into my bodysuit.

'Well, I'm just saying you should be careful. You're exposing yourself to a lot here. So make sure you get tested and when you do you get tested for everything.'

I'm too angry to even respond. I think of all the needles that have been stuck into my veins and how his audacity burns more than an anal swab inside my tight, dry rectum. Motherfucker. I pick up my pleasers, hands shaking, and ask if he wants to go out the front door or the back door. Let him out with a curt goodbye, but my eyes condemn him – why'd you fuck me if you think I'm so dirty? Reminds me of that client I had a few weeks back who bothered me to go on a date with him outside, and when I finally said I was gay to get him off my back he verbally abused me – 'Disgusting, a waste of your body, how could you do something so wrong and gross as sleep with women, disgusting, disgusting' – and then wanted to fuck me for a second time, come inside that person who was so disgusting to him, be held by arms that he couldn't respect, and all I could think was: At least have the integrity to match your words to your behaviour, to keep your precious dick out of my abominable body. If I'm so vile how can you be turned on by me? $120 is not nearly enough reimbursement for being ejaculated into twice in forty-five minutes with a sprinkling of homophobia.

I'm back in the girls' room now and I've got sharp tears of rage in the corners of my eyes and a lump in my throat. I want to go home, I hate men, but this is the last day and I need the money. Pull yourself together! You've worked through worse than this. You worked through that seven-hour booking, when you finally knew that you needed to break up with your girlfriend, as she hit you repeatedly in front of a client while you were hog-tied at the wrists and ankles, and you tried to hide your tears from him so he wouldn't know the room was being debauched but not in the way he paid for, terrified that he would notice that her violence wasn't just professional play but intimate aggression, mortified that what you were most ashamed of had seeped out of the confines of the relationship and splattered on the walls for anyone to see. You couldn't apologise copiously for whatever imagined slight you had committed – the only way to make her stop – because it would draw attention to what he was witnessing; just had to keep fake-orgasming as she left red handprints over your chest and neck, keep hoping that he would take the vibrator out of you soon and untie you, so you could tally your orgasms in pussy juice on the mirror and escape the reach of her angry hands. That was a genuinely awful night; this client has only thrown your mood, don't let it affect your earnings. What am I on? Five clients so far, $510 and it's only 4.30 p.m. I've got a booking at five; pretty sure that's what the manager said earlier. I'll quickly intro all the guys there now, there are a lot coming in today, all racing to get off before the closures, there's ten of us on, though, so it's good it's busy, and I've got time for a quick halfa, the sooner I get into another client the sooner I'll have that last client pushed further away from me by someone else's touch.

No one picks me, though, and so I've got time to delve into the fear in my mind, interrogate. What does this pandemic mean for us? What does it mean for me and the future I've so carefully crafted? How long will I be out of work for? Will I be able to sneak around and see clients privately? But with hotels closed does that mean I'll have to risk seeing them in their homes? You're allowed to go to the house of an intimate partner – are my clients intimate partners because we fuck? Does it come under 'care' because touch is a need? Is my work essential? Why are intimate family and romantic partners the only authorised exceptions to isolation? If I start fucking

181

my friends, will our relationship be more legitimate to the government? Will travel change forever? How can I deliver my pitch to my potential sperm donor now? Is being knocked up by someone overseas in the next few years unfeasible? Will I even have enough money to raise a child if sex work moves online, where there's a world of people to compete with, including celebs? I need another income but the only thing I know is in-person sex work and besides, everyone is losing their jobs now, the job market is sure to crash; who'll hire an unhireable hooker? And what about my friends? I miss them already! It's been a few weeks and communicating with them over the phone is not the same. I want to feel them shake with laughter beside me, tell them they've got sleep in the corner of their eye, tuck their tag in, lie in the grass with my head in their lap, smell the scent of their shampoo, touch their arm to get their attention in a group. And my overseas friends – who knows how long it'll be till I'm with them again? I don't care about travel for the sake of travel, adding countries to a list, but I want to spend time with those I love. My heart aches to think it's already been a year since I've seen some of them, and I've been living off the expectation of being reunited with them this year, but now . . . don't think about it. You don't want to cry at work, not on this day.

'Maddy, your reg is here, he's in room one.'

Leap up, check my face, grab some towels and a drop sheet, off down the hallway. And it's my Somali client. He's such a sweetie, only ever wants to finger me softly and fuck me even softer, so soft I feel like it's not even sex, just some quiet meditative state we're entering into together. I'm glad it's him. I couldn't handle another difficult client on the back of that douchebag.

'I brought something different today.' He hands me a package as he undresses for the shower.

'What are these?!'

'They're finger cots for when I go inside you. See? I can put them on my fingers.'

'Oh, they're like mini condoms! But why do we need them?'

'Well, I have dermatitis, and because of coronavirus I have to sanitise my hands so much at work now that my fingers are cracking and bleeding – and that might be unsafe for you.'

I take his hand from him as he is drying it. It's an ashy grey with splits all along it; it must be so incredibly painful.

'Your fingers look so sore! Have you got some good moisturiser for them? And it's good you brought those cots, not just for me, which is so considerate, but also for you – by the look of these the acidity of my pussy might sting you!'

'Yeah, I moisturise all the time but it doesn't do much.' He carefully rolls one down his index finger and I lie back in quiet anticipation, knowing I don't have to expend much energy with him. He likes to feel that I'm relaxing, having a break from hard work, and I suppose I am to a degree, because he is so kind that I don't feel like I have to be constantly on alert. I trust him, which is saying a lot for a client.

As he rhythmically fingers me and I rhythmically moan my mind wanders. To Berlin, Melbourne, Brisbane, London, Delhi, Los Angeles, New York. To friends who are struggling. In Berlin, a gay boy has gone through a rough break-up, is shattered and self-doubting. I want to lie beside him and binge-watch movies, help him regain trust in himself, comfort him just by being there. In Melbourne, one of my oldest friends has given birth to her first child, is isolated and needing help. I want to be there to watch him so she can have a much-needed nap, go grocery shopping for her, give her the support she needs. In London, a sex worker friend is having a cancer scare, has to have her new implants removed for a biopsy, is terrified by the loss of income. I want to drive her to appointments, walk her dog for her, lend her money so she knows she'll make it through. I'm a hands-on friend; what does that mean in this time when we have to be hands-off? How can I help those I love from afar? How can I do things for them? How can I know they're in pain and not go to them?

It's a kernel of sadness right inside me, and his latex fingers bump up against it, twist it inside me till I quiver with it. What a cruel world, that I can have this unasked-for touch so far inside of me and yet be denied access to those who complete me. Where is the sense in that? And this gentleness with which he touches me – does he too wish he were reaching inside someone else? Am I getting the overflow of his love for another? Are we simply poor replacements to each other, creatures driven by the need for connection and hampered by borders and class? What would this world be without borders, without nation states? How could we move among each other, and how could the hoarded wealth of prosperous nations be shared? Trafficking only exists because borders exist, and exploitation only exists because of wealth inequality. How did I come to be lying on this bed? How did other women come to be lying on other such beds? It's nearly always a tale of migration or economic need. Need that led to this symbiotic relationship I feel with him, and the parasitic relationship I feel with my wealthy clients, whereby I am leaching from them just as they leach the labour of the working class; we're both leeches in that equation and I burst with blood like a pomegranate, staining their hotel bedsheets. What does it mean that I do sex work because I am working class but am no longer working class through doing sex work? On this bed now, with a migrant man who stacks shelves, who sells the use of his body just as I sell the use of mine, where I am the product and he could physically overpower me if he wished, who has the power? Is that what this is even about, an exchange of power? That's what people always debate, who is exploiting whom; the woman either can't consent or she's manipulating the desires of the man. Is everything in life a power exchange, though? I don't think I could reduce this moment to such a simplistic take on it, and besides, I feel equal to him; whatever is between us is malleable, and flows.

His pace is getting faster and I quicken my sighs in response, should be about time to fake it so we can move on to penis penetration; he is only able to be pleased after he feels he has pleased me. What a gentleman! Don't need him to know that the sex I enjoy most with men is when they pound me hard and fast; I like a quickie and a sense of being disregarded, but only when I know there's respect behind it.

Finger cots off, condom on, and he's fucking me slowly in doggy and I back up into him to encourage him to blow, know the way my arse cheeks spread with the impact, know the way my arsehole gapes invitingly when I'm relaxed; if that isn't a sight that'll get him going I don't know what is. He wants to hold my hair like they often do, marvelling at the softness and the blondeness, and I'm a bow bent in his hands, my neck taking the strain of each thrust – hope he finishes soon or I'll end up with a pulled muscle. Though I guess that doesn't matter so much when I'm about to go into a long period without work . . .

'I'm gonna come,' I fib, and I feel his cock pulse inside me, and I think of the strength of the latex and hope it holds out no matter how big his load. A load that I'm now cradling in careful hands, carrying to the bin with a caution that bestows more value on it than its worth, as if it's something precious when really I just don't want to spill any sperm when I'm the one who has to use this room next. Some men insist on tying it up and taking it home to dispose of, as if sex workers are semen-hungry desperadoes who'll search through the trash and steal your DNA, insert it inside themselves and sue you for child support. When they do that I want to say, Mate, I do have a list of potential sperm donors and you are *not* on it.

This client isn't like that, though. He cleans himself up and then helps me to clean the room up, asks me what I'm going to do for money during lockdown, says he'll be thinking of me. I'll be thinking of you too, the money you bring me and the consideration you treat me with and your poor, painful hands. At least his job is assured – one of the lucky ones.

'There's a client waiting for you, half an hour, room three,' the manager tells me as I let my Somali client out.

'Oh yeah, easy – have I seen him before, do you know?'

'I don't think so. He just asked for whatever Western girl was on.'

Go quickly into the girls' room to grab more towels and it's empty, everyone must be in jobs. There are dressing-gowns and hair extensions and half-eaten meals everywhere, which reminds me that

I should order a burrito before I go into this next booking. Good that everyone is making money; guess there's money to be made in the destruction of society just as there is in the building of it and whores, like cockroaches, endure, because we have to. So I scuttle back down the hallway, picking up the client on the way. He's a young tradie, obviously just knocked off after a long day.

I make the bed as he showers, reach for a condom in his size as he lies down, lick his nipples as I check he's hard enough, sigh as I skewer myself onto him as if his dick is large and I've been waiting for it, it's a missing piece of me that I've pined for. He won't let me ride, though, so eager that he's fucking up from underneath me, ruining my rhythm and so, 'Doggy?' I suggest, and that's how he ends up coming in less than two minutes, panting across my back.

'That was fast.' He's a little mortified.

'That's okay, it's a compliment! Besides, easier for me, I've got a long shift today so really I should be thanking you. You've been at work too, I'm guessing?'

We get chatting and he's got a girlfriend he loves and lives with but they never have sex; she's told him he can seek it out elsewhere.

'She was raped by a guy friend of hers last year, and at first it was okay and we still fucked a lot, but

189

it's started messing with her the last few months and she's pretty off sex.'

'Man, that's so rough. It'll probably just take time. It's good you're not rushing her, though. I hope things ease up for her, and for both of you.' And I give him a kiss on the cheek, watch him walk down the stairs, going back to his love and her hurt.

Gets me thinking about all the women hurt at the hands of men. All the women raped in war, all the women who will be trapped in houses with violent partners over the coming months. I think about that young girl murdered by a client in the CBD, how her self-defence classes couldn't save her from the intent of someone bigger than her. I think of how scared she must've been in her last moments and how so many people came to know her through her death, but she isn't defined by those awful minutes of terror; her life was years of laughter before that. I think of how every day I go alone into rooms with men who are stronger than me, how vulnerable I am and how sometimes I'm scared, how that rich London girl, daughter of a 70s rock musician, said, 'But that sounds so dangerous – why would you do it?' And I didn't even know how to answer because her world was so different from mine – where to start? Because my dad isn't famous and wealthy like yours yet I want to be able to travel overseas and hang in foreign bars like you do. These are not things to be thinking of now, though, not on my last shift. If I get too anxious about what clients can do to me I'll be afraid to go into the room with them and, besides, I know men have treated me just as badly as a woman on the street, sometimes even worse. If I am killed, will my death usurp my life?

The doorbell rings and it's my dinner. Gulp down the burrito, wash my mouth out with water so I don't get chilli in my pussy after sucking some guy off, what time is it now? 6.30 p.m. so I've got a bit under six hours to go and I'm sitting on $750, that's good, I should easily make a grand tonight, which buys me two weeks in which to adjust to lock-down and figure out what the hell I'm going to do without work. This is all I've done for seven years; it's all I know! And while I'm skilled they're not skills that are recognised; they're hard to write about in a résumé. I thought I could just always do it, that sex work would always be waiting for me with clinging arms and crowded couches and sagging beds. I've contemplated moving on but thought it would be a slow transition, not that it would suddenly stop. So many people must be feeling this now, their careers vanishing.

The doorbell rings again and I intro a young guy whose cap is pulled low over his face. 'What's your nato?' His eyes peer out at me with interest.

'Australian. What about you?'

'Sri Lankan, but born here. I want to see you.'

'Okay, sick, I'll tell the manager.' And I trot back along the hallway to let her know.

He takes his hat off in the room and he's got a beautiful face. Beautiful body too; I'd probably fuck him for free if I were horny.

'You've got a good body,' I concede as I slide the condom on with my mouth. 'You work out?'

'Yeah, I box.'

'Hot.'

'What about you?'

'I swim. You Tamil or Sinhalese?'

'Tamil.' And he pushes my head down so I gag a little, just the amount I like to gag. I finger myself as he face-fucks me and I can feel my pussy swelling and pushing outwards, ready to swallow my hand if I let her, and I open my legs wider so I can rock against the edge of the bed, just as I open my throat wider to accommodate him. I'm too impatient for this. 'I want you to fuck me,' I say truthfully, and then he pushes me back on the bed without cere- mony and I'm laughing because I haven't been fucked like this in ages and I'm falling off the side of the bed and then he's picking me up and putting me on top of him but pulling me down with his arms so he's going well in me and I've got hair in my mouth and his sweat is on me and it's so rare to get a root like this at work and it's making me forget everything else momentarily as he grabs my ankles and turns me onto my stomach and enters me from behind and I can see the veins in his arms pumping as he pumps me and I think, Oh god, if only they were all like this, this job would be the best job in the world, wish he was my last booking of the day, what a one to finish on, I love fun sex not serious sex, it's a game like all good things, I want to get the same rush from it that I do from swishing on a swing set or frolicking in a field, and I arch my arse up into him so it hits a different angle, an angle that I usually keep tucked away because it can hurt but with him I want it, it reminds me of how my ex used to fuck, all flurry and feistiness so I'd forget which way on the bed was up, so I'd forget how many times I'd come or which hole they were even inside, I just want all my orifices filled by you and all your bodily fluids inside me, spit on your fingers and put them in, spit on my face and then lick the inside of my lips, let me frig against you like I'm in season, my vulva winking like a mare's with need, it's all animal, split me up the middle and stain the floor the lurid pink of your fantasies, turn me into a wet patch to argue over after, is this what the pandemic is taking away from me, my hair caught under my armpits as he shudders into my shoulders and I didn't even come but I don't care because he fucked me like the ghosts of lovers past and I won't get another one like that today, we're both gasping for breath.

'That was fun. You should come see me again if we ever reopen.'

He grins and nods, unable to speak yet, and I feel his heart thump beneath my hand and know mine is thumping the same, know it's invigorated and he fucked the fear right out of me, thanks, man, for this reminder that everything is transient, and that sometimes the best things in life are fleeting and that's okay, you'll be okay, as you always are.

friday

THE WATER IS SO COLD THAT MY NIPPLE ACHES AS IT PINCHES tight around its piercing. I'm chasing that summer feeling, where I roll from sleep into the crackle of the ocean floor around my ears, lie back in it just as I lie back in the bed, lazy and indolent, and beg a lover for orgasms. This is the closest I can get to it now, with the salt water brackish in my mouth as I duck under a wave, my limbs heavy and coagulating like the blood within me, slowly petrifying in the mid-winter temperatures. The sky is a sharp cloudless blue, not the soft monotony of high summer but a crystal glare, with the crisp branches of deciduous trees along the coastline. Serious swimmers pass me doing laps as the sunbathers give me strange looks. I'm the only girl in the water without a wetsuit, and I'm in nothing but a G-string.

They don't know that I woke with panic in my mouth, ate beta blockers for breakfast to try to ebb the flow, wanted a joint, a drink, anything, and so came here instead in the hope the shock of the cold would throw me right up out of my mind and out of myself, till I felt a different person. They don't know that I came here every day through lockdown, that it kept me sane when I wasn't allowed to see anyone, that I climbed through construction sites to avoid security guards stationed on the shut-down beaches, slithered down walls of barnacles to get into the Pacific that was denied me.

We can socialise again now. Can even go to a cafe or a sauna. Brothels are still closed, though, with no clear open date in sight, even though you can be touched by a masseuse if you want, or if you're a gay guy you can be touched by a stranger in a bathhouse – a loophole, because the government obviously hasn't realised that sex occurs in gay bathhouses. I'm fretting at the closures. Who decides what are the most high-risk activities? I want to get back to work, I need the money, wish someone would design a professional glory hole I could work with, a corona-friendly sheet of perspex with a gash in it for clients to stick their cock through, and I could back my own gash up against it so they could enter me, my cheeks spreading against the barrier with each slam, you can look but you can't touch.

That would've been genius. Instead, for the last three months I've been sneaking around in a grey area of the law, going to clients' houses, unsure if I'm risking a fine. If I can go to a friend's house to hang, and I can go to a friend's house to fuck, can I not go to a random man's house to be paid to fuck? No one really knows. The laws are mostly arbitrary and ill-defined and at the discretion of individual cops, and we all know what cops are like. The first time I left my home for a client I dressed in sportswear to seem like I was exercising and hid my condoms beneath a skipping rope, so I could claim I was just in the city to purchase it. The surveillance on the streets added to the intense scrutiny I already feel as a sex worker as I crept up the stairwell of the barristers' chambers, and he fucked me on the boardroom table with the curtains open, overlooking empty office after empty office with all those people gone, working from home. An illicit fuck made even more illicit; I was right, though, that sex work will survive anything, even a city made vacant and still.

Wish I felt vacant and still. Still got that girl on my mind. What a fool I was to get caught up in a flirtation with someone overseas in a time like this!

She's playing you, my friends say, but I know I've really played myself, went into it knowing I was susceptible and it was doomed. I've had to dig the crush from myself, tucked away behind my final rib, deeper than the emotion I felt. Have had to slide my fingers through pulp and innards to pluck it out, (have been) gutted. I want to exhume it from my soul, too, but that's proving harder. How do I wring an intangible thing? I can't even find my soul with my hands, let alone rinse it and hang it out to dry. I want to see the crush drip drip to the ground, just as the water drips from my hair to the pavement now on the walk back to my car, toes purpled with cold.

I think I'm going to be frustrated till I can make you come, she said; it was simply sext talk, though, and she won't be. But I'm going to be frustrated till I can get her out of my mind. If only I could shut her out as I'm shutting out that brisk breeze with a slam of my door. There's not much traffic about; maybe I should swing by the Habit and drop those lemons off. Two dozen that I could never get through but will be demolished in a day in that queer share house. Always nice to drop in and see who's there anyway; could be an iso aerobics class going, or a Fijian-style cook-up. It's a scrap of community left standing with all the clubs closed, the building sagging and splitting at the seams, exploding with queer bodies, black and brown and white. Where we all ended up after the huge Black Lives Matter protest, around a fire pit while cops kettled protesters into Central Station and sprayed them with capsicum spray. Strange that it took media attention on black deaths in the United States for the average white person to speak about them here — as if we haven't had blak people killed here for hundreds of years too. Is it because we consume more of the culture of black Americans than bla(c)k Australians? Do we only begin to care about marginalised people when they create art that we value, when they talk and move in ways that we deem cool?

The streets of Newtown are crowded, you could almost forget there was a pandemic if it wasn't for the fact that we're all trapped here, can't leave the state or the country, and that does something to your psyche even if you weren't planning on leaving. Knowing you can't makes the borders shrink around you, like jeans in a bath, till you feel yourself tight up against the confines, constricted. The homeless man on my street who I give weed to is back begging in the daytime, though now he has somewhere else to sleep at night, he tells me: the government has placed him in housing because of corona. Great, but what a copout; it proves we could've been housing those sleeping rough all along. It's masks-on in Melbourne though not really here; there's a complacency with the low cases and the individualistic culture. The average Australian wouldn't wear a mask to protect themselves during the bushfires; why would they wear one to protect others? Besides, 32 million HIV-related deaths couldn't convince civilians to wear condoms . . .

Man, those bloody bushfires. When I last went home I pulled over halfway to see the regeneration, psychedelic green sprouting from trunks and earth. It seemed fresher somehow after the fires, reinvigorated. The paint was still melted off all the road signs, though, and when I went to the neighbours' for a bonfire the horses they had rescued began to scream in terror; I'd never heard a horse scream like that before. Can't help thinking the regrowth is just ready to be demolished in the next round, that it's all in vain because the planet can't recuperate faster than our intent to destroy.

Why even bother with it all? The world is dying and my friends could be dead before I can see them again, anyone can die at any moment and there's nothing we can do about it – and what if I'm losing my last moments with them? Kept apart from those I love as the sand speeds through the hourglass, and who knows which days in particular are numbered? If I could delete myself from life and people's memories I would; I've seen what grief can do to people, though, and I never want to inflict that on anyone, that's the thread which holds me here some days: not wanting to hurt my friends. So I still plan for the future, because I know I'll push through even if I don't want to, because I have to. And at some point I'll feel good again, even if for now I'm just going through the motions, parking my car, walking down the alley, opening the side gate and –

'Heyoooo, who's around? I brought you guys some lemons.'

And there's a bunch of people sitting in a semicircle in the sun, with pyjama pants rolled up to catch the rays and fingers clutching ciggies.

'Perfect timing, we were just about to smoke a joint – you want some?' a trans girl says, and I gesture to her to stay seated as she gets up to greet me with a kiss.

'Love that you're single-handedly bringing back cold-calling,' another girl quips, shaking her dykey do so it falls around her face like Leonardo DiCaprio in the 90s.

'Yeah, I'll have some, nothing else to do today. May as well be stoned in the arvo.'

'Here, babes.' A boy who doesn't live there but drifts through hands me the joint. 'What have you been up to?'

'Really nothing, just smoking and masturbating and getting emotionally involved with a girl on the other side of the world and being devo about it – corona things.'

'That's so lesbian: long distance and yearning,' the other lesbian drawls through a drag.

'It is, but don't you reckon iso culture is, like, lesbian culture? You know, baking sourdough and tending plants and taking up crafts and stuff?'

'Not me, babes, I've been having lockdown orgies.'

'Yeah, but you're gay and a good-time gal. I'm not talking about you; I'm talking about straight people discovering what lesbians have been doing since forever.'

'If we get corona from anyone it'll be you, you're basically a walking hot spot,' the trans girl remarks to the boy as she gets up to go inside.

'Yeah, coz I'm hot and a spot people want to go to!'

'Byeee, Felicia.' She waves as she steps over the threshold without even a glance back at us.

We all sit in silence, soaking up the sun, as the plants do beside us, their little leaves opened up wide in thankfulness for the day. It is a beautiful day; there are beautiful moments in all of this. I have to remind myself of that, instead of wallowing in my heartache. I must begin to learn from my experiences and not just self-flagellate with them. In the past, I've bent over backwards in a sacrificial arc and torn the offal from my torso all to prove (I loved you) and to please. I must learn and unlearn: to give of myself without losing myself; to assert myself without fear; not to hinge my love upon the seesaw sway of a power imbalance but to step into the relationship as an equal rather than as a combatant already cowed and apologetic. Surely I can love truly, passionately, sincerely, respectfully without throwing myself in as the greatest offering. Twenty-fucking-seven years old and I can say this sub rosa, whispered into the ear of a lover, but can I actually carry it out with them?

'Honestly, romance is a trap. I think I'm done with it forever. Like, I never want to date or get involved with someone again. It just makes me unhappy.'

'You're only in your twenties, all my relationships in my twenties were bad — wait till your thirties. I think having a break from it all and being single for a few years till you break whatever pattern you're in is a good idea, though.' Wisdom in her words and her fingers as she stubs out the joint.

The huge eucalyptus overhanging us begins to creak and we all leap up fast, the boy exclaiming, 'Babes, I'm getting out of here before that widow maker drops something on my head!' and she adds, 'Yeah, I'm gonna go have a nap.'

Guess that's the end to the conversation then, and I'll head home. I'm feeling pretty slug; better to be feeling that than anxious. And, actually, a little bit horny; press my hand against my crotch as I sit in the driver's seat to test how much. Definitely enough that I could be bothered straining my RSI wrist, can spread-eagle on my couch and luxuriate in a slow wank, heightened by the weed. Have to make sure I don't think of her, though; it'll just solidify the feelings I'm trying to move on from.

Meander slowly home, cutting through the grounds of Sydney Uni to avoid the traffic – that's my right as an alumna, isn't it? Who can I think of that's not dangerous territory? Porn doesn't work for me; my mind inevitably shifts to someone from my life. I can only get off to people who I know are or have been sexually interested in me, get off on their attraction as much as my own, imagine myself through their eyes touching me, a true bottom. I'm driving with one hand on the steering wheel and the other lazily bumping against my pussy, conjuring up memories and shifting through them, rejecting exes as unhealthy. Maybe work memories are the safest. I've had lots of fun fucks with male clients, but none that I savour afterwards, want to taste on my tongue again. Men slather me in compliments and sometimes make me come and it's all dust to me, doesn't touch the real of my real, the part of me that's wanted to woo women and be wooed by them, has wanted to pour the contents of my heart into a vase and present it, a pretty rose-coloured trinket, to the obscure object, has wanted to roll them up into a neat little ball and press it flat with my eager palms on her school desk, so she could read it and know how much I pledged, has wanted to string them up in neon lights so she could look out at night and see not the stars but my devotion.

Here I am in my lounge room, naked from the waist down because it's too cold to be totally naked, licking the salt off my arm as I slowly stroke my clit, and I'm thinking of the middle-aged couple who book me, the man rich and the woman hot, with 80s curls and a rock climber's taut rig that she keeps beneath mum jeans, because she is a mum. I think of how he pays me to fuck her while he watches, and how sometimes he helps but sometimes he can't overcome his whisky dick, or sometimes he's watching over FaceTime while on a plane, travelling for business. I think of her abs, slick with coconut oil, and her tribbing my thigh and the quick little sounds she makes as my tongue is against her and she gets closer to orgasm. I think of that time when I made her come with a combination of Hitachi and fingers and he asked me to stay for another hour for $600, and I broke the code of whore's tact and said, 'To be honest, I'm actually really excited to go home and fuck my girlfriend so I can't, but this has been great foreplay,' and how he was taken aback but she was touched. And then I went home and my girl-friend ripped my stockings open and fisted me from behind till I let out a primal howl like I usually only do in anal, when my body is so overstimulated that my throat lets go . . . not that memory!

Then what about that woman client who came in to the massage parlour when I'd just broken up with my other girlfriend and was crying over her in the girls' room. Bottle blonde, tight black leather pants and ankle boots, a red sweater, gorgeous face. The other girls all gushed, 'Why isn't she on this side of the counter?' I didn't think she'd pick me; she was high femme and hot, and what did I have to offer her? I'm not attractive to women! I was so nervous in the room that my hands were shaking, hesitant to touch her. Did she want, like, asexual body sliding? Or did she want to orgasm? Or, like, was she not even okay with this and oh my god I shouldn't even be touching her because maybe she doesn't want this even though she's paid for this?! 'Ummm, so, do you want me to touch you? Coz I'm happy to – I mean I would like to – but I don't want to do anything you're not comfortable with.' We ended up fucking and it was wonderful and that's a special memory to me, because it came at one of my lowest points and was like the universe telling me, You will be all right, you will connect with people again, you will come back into yourself after feeling like only a husk of a human after an abusive relationship.

I've stopped fiddling with myself as I think of that, though. It takes me to too many other painful memories. Such as having an unpaid threesome with my ex a few days after I had broken up with her for hitting me, because while we were still together we had brokered a deal with an unethical lawyer for him to represent her for her DUI charge in exchange for three hours of our time, a deal that neither of them would release me from and is the only time I have felt really coerced into sex, with no way out and no cash consolation. Quid pro quo more like quid pro no.

Come on, reel your mind back in. What else is in the vault? How about that woman who grew up in the USSR, the one with the greenest eyes I'd ever seen and Soviet-style tatts down her back? The one who fucked me with the strap-on I brought to the booking and was soft to kiss and I wanted her to stay longer but felt pathetic asking a client, when I've always looked down on people who could fall for a client, to hang with me afterwards. I want to kiss her again, I want to be topped by her again, I want to befriend her like I do every cool and interesting girl. Fuck, it'd be hot if she booked me again – my quim quivers around my index. And what about that girl who was like my teen dream come to life, all curves and red pubic hair, and I ate her pussy while her partner fucked me from behind, knew his place like all good stunt dicks, and I could smell her on me in the elevator as I left.

There's also that seven months' pregnant woman who had never slept with a girl before but whose pregnancy hormones made her want to try it and whose husband left the house to accommodate us. I had never been up close to a pregnant woman and I'd certainly never fucked one. Her breasts were firmer than silicone implants, blue veins showing through the pale. I held her belly in awe. She felt no different inside from any other woman; I expected it to be different somehow. The way my pussy clenches now, though, feels just as hers did then. I felt a reflected glow from her, imagined myself pregnant through my partner's eyes, finding splendour in the same things I was finding splendour in. God that was hot. More than hot, though, it was transcendental. I may not have a partner anymore but I can't wait to be pregnant. I'd offer myself up to a select few, profit off the pregnancy financially, sure, but that's just work and meaningless – what I really want is to give those I like the experience that was given to me, passing my fecund body into their hands with trust and desire. Will she want to fuck me when I'm like that? Not supposed to be thinking of her now but I'm a glutton, can't help myself, and I'm so close to orgasm, think of her fingers teasing my labia beneath a restaurant table, think of her looking into my eyes and asking if I want more, think of her pushing me up against the wall of a laneway, pulling up my skirt and fucking me fast because we're too impatient to make it back to her apartment and privacy. I think I'm going to be frustrated till I can make you come, she said. You're making me come now, though; I'm wet down to my wrist and there's going to be dried cum along with the dried salt on my skin.

Damn. That was so good. But maybe I shouldn't have done it. It was kind of a step backwards and, besides, what are the ethics of masturbating over someone who probably isn't into you? Oh well. Maybe it's only inappropriate if you tell them you did. This is between my pussy and me. And my mind – that organ which lusts after emotional connection more than anything else. How do I reconcile the romantic part of me with the pragmatic? What did that boozy tarot reader slur at me over a pack of cards and a glass of white in Enmore the other day? I need to bring the two sides of me that are at war together. But how do I do that? Do I clip one to fit the other?

I want to nurture someone, and the something between us, yet I don't trust my taste in people, or myself in relationships. I bristle and burr with boundaries to protect my heart and as soon as I feel I am getting into someone I panic, which then fulfils my own prophecy that romance is bad for me. I want and I'm scared and I feel weak for wanting. I've tried romance a number of times, and Einstein says stupidity is trying the same thing again and again and expecting different results – so who's the idiot here? Better just to stick to friends and casual sex than risk the complete and utter destruction which comes with that kind of vulnerability and sacrifice. Fuuuuuck that.

So I tangle with my dreams and myself. Wrestle with them bare-handed till my wrists are a crisscross of scratches. Attempt to get that clinging vine under control, that goddamn weed that climbs through my visions. I know I don't need it, but I want it. (Why? Am I so brainwashed? Is it human nature?) And you can't have it, because that would be a very bad idea. Yes I'm speaking to myself like a child because I need to be spoken to like that. Have to slap my own hand away from my phone when I go to text her: don't indulge the fantasy. You know what you want from life and being involved with someone only complicates things. Be an ascetic about this. Practise emotional celibacy.

For how long, though? Till I've broken whatever pattern I'm in? Till I have children? Till I'm thirty-five? Till I meet the right person? I don't believe in that. It's an ongoing journey, the tarot reader said, there's no clear end. What was her name again? She had some epic Australian pun. Laurie something. Laurie Keet! That was it. Press my hand against my cunt; she still has that post-orgasm feel. Should clean her up, clean myself up, do something with the last of the day. Could wander down to the park, look over the graffitied sandstone cliffs to the harbour, chat to the teen bong rats pulling cones in the cracks. Could climb the Moreton Bay figs that stink of flying fox. Could play on the swings till my blisters burst. I'm feeling okay now that I'm sun drunk and high. Could almost forget the pervasive low, it's gone, swiped like smegma from my hood, excised from my soul; I sneezed out the sickness like a cold.

That's what I think right now, but later today or tomorrow morning it will have come back with a vengeance, or before my period with a vendetta, ready to shed blood both from my lining and in conflict. I pick fights to appease the chaos within me; a black hole of insecurity and need and an anger I never feel at other times. The world is a mess and so am I. Am I too much of a mess for her? Has my mental health driven her away? You're most attractive when you're confident, my ex said to me; once you start to show your vulnerability it's a turn-off. That's a bit of a catch 22; means I'm bound to deter people as soon as I begin to give a fuck. Am I destined, then, to careen through life fucking people I don't care about and crying in the girls' room over ones who don't like me the way I like them, coming up with an allergy rash from the dusty pillows? How is all of this bigger to me than the world ending? Am I inherently selfish, or is the world ending exacerbating the rejection, or am I leaning into it to distract from the world ending?

Moving on from an internet fling is more difficult than I realised. With in-person things you can avoid the physical spaces that remind you of them, like the bar where you met or the cafe you used to go to together. When it's online, though, it's like they only existed in your mind – and how the hell do you get them out of there? Why did no one warn me? People always demean online relationships as less legitimate, phone sex as not counting, the emotions only a mockery of the real; when your mind is what you live in, though, surely bringing someone to live in there with you can mess you up as much as living with someone in the literal sense?

The sun is already starting to go down and with it my mood. No point going to the park now; there'll be a chill in the air with the breeze coming off the harbour and my fingers will freeze on the play equipment. The sun setting means she's starting to stir, and my anxiety is on the rise because now if she doesn't reply to me it's not because she's asleep but because she doesn't want to or I'm not on her

215

list of priorities or she's over talking to me or she's just over me as a person and I'm a gnat buzzing her phone up and she'd rather I just didn't. Why did I ever get involved with her? Lockdown was the perfect environment for obsession to rot; with no outside distractions my mind turned inwards and preyed upon itself.

Erghhh, I hate myself when I'm like this, so self-absorbed and indulgent. Reading over texts I've sent, wondering how I could've phrased them differently, how I could've crafted myself to be the cool girl that I'm obviously not and never will be because I feel my emotions loudly and am far too forthright, and besides I don't even like reserved people, so why in these moments do I wish I was one? What if I'd never admitted I liked her, pretended to be chill, hadn't shown that side of myself, never sent that text, never opened up, only been flippant and upbeat, not been demanding, not turned to her for comfort, just kept it casual like I said I would and thought I could – would we be somewhere different? Conditional clauses can send you mad. The happy of the high is disintegrating fast, my stomach is churning and I just want to take a Seroquel so I can pass out and wake up tomorrow feeling maybe better, maybe not.

Is it even her I care about, or am I just fixating on my most apparent failing right now? Falling short of 'enough', whether that be not good enough, not funny enough, not pretty enough, not interesting enough, not smart enough – but whose measurements are they? My own: no one else is sizing me up by them. We should appraise ourselves based on our pros not our cons. I can apply that principle to others but not to myself; I feel entirely cons, a constellation of them as pervasive and unreachable as the pimples on my back, the acne of someone who works a physical job, has people sweat onto her in doggy and can't scrub it off till ten hours later.

I need a new perspective. I need out of this house and this state (of mind). I want to feel good again for longer than the length of an orgasm or the blur of a joint. I need to leave Sydney again but there's nowhere to go. Can only go to the park at the end of my street and close my eyes on the swings and pretend I'm on a swing far away, where I'm no longer sad. Escape like I did last week.

I went home on a whim to put 530 kilometres between myself and how I was feeling; I'm that girl who runs from things, got those long legs that flee from a room when someone raises their voice, got those fidgety hands that splice the split ends of my hair, got that impatient bruxism that leaves the inside of my cheeks mush. Got that panicked attitude, gotta get gotta get out of gotta get out of here stat, that propelled me to London this time last year to get away from this city and wanting to kill myself. I've seen my mental health as largely situational, contextual, something that's not a part of me but just a reaction to stressors. I abstain from those things that I know make it worse — uppers, alcohol, lack of sleep, romantic relationships — and yet I still have days when I wake soaked in melancholy, a blue so deep I could drop right into it, fill my airways with it, have no way out. I grow increasingly frustrated with my mind. Can't you see I'm caring for you? You've got nothing legit to be sad about! Why can't I rely on you like I can my body? A 530-kilometre drive and I'm still stuck with you. Eight years on and I still think about cutting when I feel bad. Am I forever going to be defined by my lowest moments, forced to live alongside them, accept them even? I want to do better, be better. Not just for my own sake but so I can give more to the world.

I went home on a whim to wake up somewhere different, so I could feel something different, and felt happy, felt at peace, felt effervescent, but it's all just evanescent and the downs feel as if they carve a permanence into my skin. I'm that girl who wants to slip out of her own mind, tabula rasa, be simpler, feel a feeling with no fear that it'll last too long or get in the way of doing things, brush it off rather than catch in it. I'm that girl who runs physically because I can't run mentally but it's all there, rattling around inside me and bruising my soul. My anxious, needy, fretting mind that I alternate between coddling and slapping. Wake up to how good you have it, be resilient, fight alongside me not against me, *goddamn*!

saturday

MY APPETITES ARE COMING BACK. I'M BOTH HUNGRY AND horny for the first time in months. I want to dance for someone I love on a foreign street in the rain, I want to flash my kitty at passers-by while I do, I want the rain to dampen my dress and my flanks and then my pubic hair. I want them to stroke my clit to size afterwards so that I'm doubly dampened.

I want someone to slap-grab my thigh as if it's a prize leg of ham and they're weighing up its girth. I want to drool while they fuck me in the arse coz it's too much too much too much and my lips give way. I want a smorgasbord of sex. I want a charcuterie board too which I can't even say, but I'll eat it.

I want to dine at a restaurant without checking the prices on the menu. I want to be spoilt but not spoiled, I want to be spent, loins soaked and cum smears, gasping for breath across someone I'm into, reaching for the glass of water bedside. I want to stay in that bed all morning. I want to hold hands.

I want to scream at a cloudless blue sky, beautiful in its monotony. I want to swim along the ocean floor and come up with seaweed in my hair. I want someone to drink brine from between my legs like it's sake, and then drink me. I want to sip elder-flower lemonade.

I want to see friends who only exist in my phone. I want better for everyone everywhere. I want people not to be killed anymore. I want the earth to survive us.

I want to sleep without medication for the first time in six years. I want that client to book me again. I want to kiss lips softer than my own. I want to rub against someone like a cat in heat so they come away smelling of me. I want to laugh, always. I want to live.

I'm getting one of those things, at least. Here I am at the nude beach. Not the mixed nude beach – the gay nude beach. It's all hairy chests and taut buttocks, and teeny Speedos darting across the sand as the ice-cream boat pulls in and all the men stroll over to purchase an overpriced Golden Gaytime. I like being here because I don't get watched or followed or creeped on in the bushes – and besides, I'm a fag hag and a dyke, where else would I belong? I like watching a gay threesome happening on one of the docked boats just as much as anyone else here, just wish I had a boat and could put on my own display. Lesbian sex doesn't get nearly the public stage it should except in porn; where's our exhibitionism? We curl up with each other in bed instead and tend to plants and buy a pink salt lamp and gift a scoby to a couple who've just moved in together and stop going out till all the lesbian bars close. We're out in our lives but not out on the beaches, not like the gays with their knees sandy from giving a gobby at Lapa, a prime place for it with a pristine view. I should be a tour guide for sure: let me show you the ten best beaches for whatever dirty deed you have in mind. It's not dirty here, though, not with this backdrop; it's wholesome and natural and, yes, cum is vegan too. Just don't litter, that's the only no-no.

I slip beneath the surface, still like the Mediterranean in this hidden cove, gently rocking waves that hardly break, and there's a cormorant a few feet from me that dives again and again, popping up where I least expect him, feathers slicked back like the pomaded hair of a mechanic. I can see the city across the harbour, know that as my sight travels there so does my sound, from when we used to have raves in the deserted World War II bunkers with their low concrete ceilings perfect for heavy techno and packed bodies. We'd lie munted on the grass surrounds, make out with each other, take a coming-up shit in the bushes near the zoo, scatter when the cops came to shut us down after noise complaints from all the way across the other side of the water. When I first moved to Sydney and saw the orange glow of the sky at night instead of ink and stars I cried, felt sick from the light pollution; by the time these parties rolled around I saw it differently. 'The sky is pink coz I'm in love!' I exclaimed to a friend as we smashed through a pack of ciggies. I'd made the city mine by then and loved its idiosyncrasies.

Just as I love it now, can hardly believe that as Melbourne friends risk fines for leaving their homes after curfew I can be here, free to move as I wish, naked in the sun, my only worry that I might burn my pale punani; she's unused to the rays. Sydney, I love you! And I love you, pelican, don't choke on that fish you're downing; and I love you, water, and the way you caress between my legs, know that my vagina will vacuum you up only to gush you out later on unsuspecting clients, a trick she likes to play on tricks: they think I've squirted when really I've just let go; and I love you, gay boy posing for a photo on the prow of that boat and – wait a second, he looks familiar . . .

'Oi! Marcus!'

'Oh my god, babe, what are you doing here? Come on board!'

I swim out to them and clamber nude up the ladder and there's a bunch of boys lounging over empty oyster shells and glasses of prosecco. What a vibe and what a city to be single in, one where you can live that sylph life, float through others' nautical parties and leave their lashes curled behind you, tip tilted from the airflow of your swift exit. They offer me a drink and a joint but I take only a strawberry. I've got a booking later, I say, have to be alert for that.

'Oh, are you working again?'

'Yeah, the broths have reopened, thank god. I've been doing two or three shifts a week. It's been kinda busy coz a lot of girls haven't come back . . .'

I pause as I think of how smashed we were that first week. Our clients had months' worth of blue balls but there were only half the girls we usually had. By the third day of it we were tired but, as the Chinese girl next to me and I agreed, we had to work because what if we went into lockdown again? *Don't*

227

feel like working today, she said to me, and when I said, *Babe, I feel you*, she quipped, *I tell them my pussy leaving at home, I forget my pussy today, baby, have to let me go home*, and we both laughed till an intro was called and we had to steady our faces.

'. . . But today I've got a private with a reg. And he's paying me extra for a golden shower and anal so I wanna be at my most professional, you know how it is.'

'How often do you do those?'

'Well, funny you should ask that, coz I've only started doing anal again recently. I'll always do golden showers if I'm asked but I'm always hesitant with anal coz I worry about getting hurt if they're too rough. But then I did some rogue anal a few months back after not doing it for years and remembered how much I like it and what good value it is for money coz the guys come so fast. As long as their dick isn't big it's easy.'

'I only do it when their dick is big, but I'm doing it for pleasure not business. Size queen.' He looks smug as he ashes over the side of the boat.

They're having the time of their lives and it's tempting to stay but I have to get going, I've got that booking, and so I air kiss them goodbye and dive off the side of the boat and swim to shore and then drip dry as I climb the shadowed path to the car park, all the while thinking about what got me doing anal again, how I was sobbing in the armchair in the girls' room because not getting picked in the intros reinforced my rejection: she didn't want me and now neither did these razzo guys. Work was meant to be a distraction but instead it made me feel worse, till I ended up on my knees crying. I'd given up on looking good, given up on self-respect, given up on being desirable because I wasn't desirable to her. Amazing how an unreciprocated crush can rock your self-esteem so much. Amazing and terrifying and all the more reason to avoid crushes entirely. Look where it leaves me: pathetic and unable to work. Maybe you should skip this intro, my manager said. You've got a booking with a reg in halfa anyway, the only booking you'll get today because you're too tragic otherwise. (She didn't actually say that last bit but she could've; it would've been true.) And I went into the room and it was the client who likes to put a blindfold on while he fucks me, which I was grateful for coz he wouldn't see my swollen eyes, and we have this established role play where he pounds me in doggy and I beg to be allowed to touch myself, please, master, please may I come? And he rubs his cock on my arsehole while I whimper and say it's too big for me. But that time I wanted to be taken outside of myself, do something outside my usual, and so while he was doing his normal anal tease I said just put it in, in the same tone in which I would say to a friend let's get fucked up, all resolute and reckless, and he was shocked and hesitated, said really, and I said yep, just put heaps of lube on, and then he eased in slowly and for the first time I had sex in which I wasn't thinking of her, coz it was slutty and impersonal and I'd never thought of her taking me that way and I came so fucking hard and then I said sorry but I'll have to ask for $100 extra for that, I know I didn't say that before we did it, didn't mean to scam you, and he said that's fine I have cash on me, I didn't realise you do anal though, and I said neither did I really, but now I do – and that's something this round of obsession has brought me, more cash, so grateful for that.

Weird the things that heartache will take you to – won't say heartbreak, because it wasn't really that: the manic decisions madly made to get out of your mind. The way that Indian boy sought me out for a wristy and spurt of sperm, and ended up just talking about her anyway because he carried her with him still, folded up nice and neat in the bureau of his brain, couldn't access any memory without reaching over her to retrieve it. What was the advice I gave him? Be transparent; find out what the other wants before you invest. Why couldn't I listen to my own advice? Maybe it wouldn't have helped, though. I've always thought honesty begets honesty but I was wrong. Seems some people enjoy the ambiguities, the prevarications, the maybes, the somewheres in between that allow for all possibilities – if they give no clear answer they can flip and turn in those spaces, knowing that nothing has been ruled out. I certainly have no elusiveness in me, only frankness (I like you, do you like me at all that way? Would you like to fuck me some time?); I ask directly to allow them an easy no, but I've learnt that some people feel trapped by the directness, and that baring your-self is not beautiful to all. For some there is nothing alluring in clarity; it is the greys that add tone and depth and poetry.

What would I say to him now, if he came to me again in a fevered state, desperate for any balm to ease the pain? Would I say you could behave strictly by your own moral code and still not account for how another behaves? Would I utter clichés like 'I would rather have loved fully than not at all' and 'love conquers all', sentiments that leak like faulty taps through the narratives of romance that we consume, that we sicken on, that even with my eyes open I drank and drank and still wondered why I choked? Would I say focus on your friendships, they are the true relationships to foster? Would I say whatever, love sucks and hurts and we go back to it again and again and that's a part of life and we just have to work out how to minimise that hurt coz all vulnerability is a risk really. I thought I was wise, was in a position to give him helpful advice, when really I'm just cynical and at the mercy of my moods as much as anyone. Not as stoic as I would wish, Libra moon a bruise within me.

Okay, made it home, what have I gotta do? Shower, shave my legs, eat, check I've got the right-sized condoms. Drive to his place in peak hour. God, how I miss the roads of home, the blind corners and burn-out marks and even the loose gravel with dust clouds rising. The way the solar power cuts out at midnight and the music stops, and the way we huddle around the battery-powered radio with the kerosene lamps lit as if it's the 30s, listening to the broadcasts. Heard the news of Trump's corona diagnosis crackle over the channel in the pitch-black, fixed the antenna to hear it more clearly, knew I was part of a significant moment in history that was lent a timelessness by the medium. Get the genny going, one of the other girls said. But if we'd powered up that petrol gulper we never would have heard this, that elocution lesson voice reaching out across the verandah to touch the edges of the rainforest, stirring the leaves; we would've read it solitarily on our phones instead of having the knowledge hit us all at once, dousing us in this illness of global interest.

The rainbow lorikeets are screeching in the back-yard as I slurp some spaghetti and I think of all the voice notes I've sent to people, how when I relisten to them I can hear the parrot screams and magpie warbles in the background, how there's a stamp of Australiana on every missive I send out into the world that a European would never recog-nise but which pierces an Australian living overseas with nostalgia and the scent of eucalyptus in the rain, how that's more beautiful than any confession of feeling or apology that I've stumbled over, that tropical chorus – we've got more types of parrots than the Amazon, did you know? It's about the only thing that makes me feel patriotic, that and being the fastest English language speakers in the world, try and outpace me, I dare ya.

I need to pick up my pace now – get going, girl. It's five o'clock already and you've gotta be ready ringing at his doorbell at six with a clean arsehole and a bladder full of pee. Take that pineapple juice to finish off in the car, let's go.

This client's such a breeze, a widower, been seeing him for five years now, she passed seven years ago. He knows the ins and outs of my life, calls me by my real name yet never oversteps a boundary. As he opens the door to me he asks how's it going with that girl overseas, and I remember that last time I was here I was at the height of it, exhilarated by the flirtation and high off orgasms, talking to him about my infatuations as I always do.

'Oh right, yeah, that. Wow, that feels so long ago. She ended up not being into me. It got a bit confusing. I was devo for ages but I feel fine now,' I say as I unlace my boots.

'That's a shame; it sounded like you guys had such a good connection.' And he sets a champagne flute out on the table for me to pee into – not all of it, though! Have to save some for his face in the shower. I know the routine after all these years.

'I mean, we did and we do, but it's a connection that's better as friends coz she wasn't feeling it, you know. Also, it confirmed to me once again that I am much happier and a better person when I'm not into someone. I need to stay away from that stuff for a long time. It's the friendship that mattered more to me anyway and that's why I got so into her, too, coz there was already a strong base there, so, like, nothing lost.' I fumble at the buttons of his shirt as I begin to kiss him.

Move through the motions and the rooms. Undress in the living room, my hand stirring up his cock, put a condom on, suck him for a bit. Guide him to the bedroom, my bare feet slapping on the wooden floors. His wife gazes down on us and I think of how familiar her face has become to me, how he must lose more of her each day and mourn the blurring of her features but I've gained them, how sometimes I make direct eye contact with her while I ride him and I wonder. I know the things he does with me he used to do with her and I am simply a stand-in. She was a hot kinky bitch and she also liked girls; she would've liked you, he's always said. I think of us all fucking and I think of that brothel client who masturbated while he sobbed to the videos of a porn star who killed herself, how he paused it on a face cum shot and said this is how I'll always remember her, and I think of how people say you're still alive while someone still remembers you, and the space is suddenly a phantasmagoria of dead women, with silvered shifting outlines and mouths open for eternal swallows, I guarantee girls in the afterlife don't spit, maybe they spit roast though, I feel like purgatory would be full of group sex, perhaps she's getting off just as I'm getting off now as his cock is in my arse, damn that makes me come fast. We leave her behind as we go to the bathroom, or maybe we don't, maybe she's light-footed beside me, crouching in the corner as I squat above him aiming my stream, watching him wank till he's done. He wipes his face with a bath towel as I hop in the shower and say that was fun, and I mean it.

'Yeah, it was. I'm probably not going to be able to see you for a while – that's why I wanted to do anal today.'

'Oh really, why?'

And he tells me how he's met someone and he wants to give it a go with her. How she's Taiwanese and a working girl and how he would never have thought to date a working girl before, would've been made jealous by it, but after years of knowing me and seeing how I spoke about my girlfriends he knows that people can do this work and even sometimes enjoy it and still love their partner. How it's no reflection on their romantic relationships, and he's proud of how hard she works and that she sends money home to her family. How he would never have had this attitude if it wasn't for me, how he is grateful to me, but he wants to do the right thing by her and not see other people at the moment. I'm touched. Sure, I'll miss the money and maybe I'll even miss the sex, but what are those things compared to him finding someone he wants to be with, and her finding the same? I say farewell to him with a kiss on the cheek and a more solemn internal goodbye to his wife.

Walking back to my car a text comes through from a friend, responding to a message I sent earlier asking if she wants to hang tonight. She says she's at the Crix, can I pick her up so we can go back to mine? Perf. She's probably a little tipsy given she's at a pub but whatever, she's a buoyant drunk, I envy her that.

And we're hurtling along Wattle Street as she tells me about her exhausting six-day working week. Like everyone she's both relieved she has work during the pandemic and scared it'll disappear suddenly. All the people who thought they had secure jobs, who looked down on me and asked when I planned to leave sex work because 'you can only do it for so long', have seen their industries gutted and are retraining, whereas my work has lasted, because one thing you can count on is people will always be horny.

We're stopped at some traffic lights and a ute pulls up next to us, and I can see that the passenger is eyeing her off.

'That guy next to us is checking you out.'

'He's kinda hot.'

And so I wind down the window.

'Do I know you?' he calls. 'You look familiar.'

'No.' She somehow manages to make the word both two syllables and coquettish, and as she says it the lights change and I shoot off.

The ute is coming up the other side of the car and he asks for her name as we cruise past Wentworth Park.

'Where do you live?'

'Leichhardt. You?'

'Glebe.'

There's cars getting between us, though, and now the ute's a bit ahead and what's she going to do? They didn't even get each other's full names. I can catch up to him, I reckon, even with this Saturday night traffic.

'Have you got a pen and paper to write your number on?' I swing around the corner at full speed, overtaking two cars in one go, the stench of the fish markets sharp in my nose as I draw closer to them.

'No, I've got nothing.' She's rifling through her bag as I see the ute ahead of me, going up the ramp to the Anzac Bridge.

'Maybe you can just shout your number to him?'

We're on the bridge now and I'm switching across the four lanes, coming up alongside him again and –

'Wait, I've got an old business card!'

She gestures to him and I keep pace with the ute as she leans out the window and hands the driver her business card. What an iconic 80s move. Forget about meeting people online – nothing can beat the chemistry of in person, and I have so much adrenaline from the chase that I'm as excited as she is when her phone begins to ring as we go up Victoria Road. I don't hate love, I just hate being hurt and I hate being stressed and I'd rather no love than those things. That's okay, though, because I get enough as it is and there is so much to look forward to. So much fun to be had, so many friends to make and keep, and at some point, who knows when, but sometime, I'll see the ones separated from me by borders, and when I do I'll say let me hold your hand so I know you're not a hallucination or a figment of my imagination, after all this time, finally, I'll never take touch or travel for granted again, don't let go even if your palm is sweaty, I'm not one for affection but

I won't shirk your hug coz I'm fiending that physical contact, frothing it, I've been alone in my mind but I'm not alone in life, photograph us in this place so we know we've been someplace together, speak Polari to me, teach me to sign, unburden yourself at the door when you shed your scarf, let me look after you just as you've looked after me, I want all that and more. This is a love letter to friendship, I want you to write it on me in ink and then press me against the pages, your personal printing press. I want you to hold my ankles tight so it doesn't smudge and sign it from all of us, because without youse there's no me.

I want to wake up tomorrow feeling as good as I do today. I want this day and this drive to never end. I want the laughter to keep going, into the next and the next and the next.

I want to dance in a club. I want to cup someone's face. I want to be texted back as quickly as I text back. I want to lie beside someone for so long that I forget that they're another person and think I'm talking to myself. I want a friend to race ahead of me at a crowded market so I'm left actually talking to myself.

I want free education and health care and housing for everyone everywhere. I want to feel better so I can do better, for the world and everyone in it. I want us to slow if not halt if not reverse the effects of climate change.

I want to read out loud to someone till my mouth gets dry. I want to give a child a piggyback. I want to climb a tree. I want to skip down a pavement scuffing my toes. I want to choke because I've eaten a meal too fast and I want to laugh when I do.

I want to hang a picture. I want to smell a book. I want to cradle a cat as if it's a baby. I want to go into love boldly, like I do everything else. I want to not be incapacitated by it. I want to learn, always. I want to live.

ACKNOWLEDGEMENTS

THANK YOU TO MY AGENT GABY NAHER, THE FIRST PERSON to read this and who saw enough in it, even in the messy first draft stage, to take me on. Thank you to Jane Palfreyman, Tessa Feggans, Ali Lavau and anyone else at Allen & Unwin who was a part of turning this from notes on my phone to word docs to a book you can hold in your hands at a bookstore. Thank you to all of the creatives whose work has influenced my own and who I reference obliquely or directly. And thank you to all the readers who have followed my writing online for so many years, who have engaged with me and had faith in me and supported me—I hope the wait was worth it.